D1287560

Addicted

A *Club Destiny* Novella

Nicole Edwards

Cover Photo: © Branislav Ostojic | Dreamstime.com

ISBN: 978-0-9850591-5-6

Chapter One
~~ ** ~~ ** ~~ ** ~~

"So let me get this straight." Sam trailed her fingernail down the center of Logan's chest, enjoying the way his breath caught when she went just past his sexy as hell belly button. "You want to bring another man into our bed."

Trailing her finger back up, through the soft, dark hair spattered on his chest, she veered to the right and let her nail scrape gently over his nipple.

"That's what I'm saying." He confirmed although he didn't sound nearly as confident as Sam was used to.

This was the man who had ordered her pleasure back when Logan included his twin brother Luke in their little soirees. Since Luke had to go off and fall in love, Sam and Logan had shared some intimate conversations about who they might be able to invite to join them in the future, but had yet to venture past the talking point. Tonight she'd been the one to bring it up.

"And you've already selected someone?" She asked as she maneuvered her body so she was leaning on one elbow while still teasing him with her hand.

This time when she trailed down his chest, she dipped her finger into his navel before exploring a little lower, her hand brushing ever so slightly against the swollen head of his penis.

"Sam." Logan's voice had lowered an octave or two in warning, but Sam didn't mind. This was what she lived for.

"Yes?" She asked innocently, turning her palm against the mushroomed head and wiping the moisture from the tip.

Sitting up fully, Sam took it upon herself to remove the t-shirt she was wearing, swiftly slipping it over her head and tossing it to the floor.

"You were telling me about this man you were going to invite. Is he as hot as you are?" She asked, not actually caring but doing her best to get her husband worked up.

"I couldn't tell you that." Logan sucked in a breath when she wrapped her hand around his shaft, the feel of satin coated steel beneath her palm.

"Sure you can." She said as she glided her hand up and then down, barely gripping him. He liked when she teased him, and more importantly, Sam liked what came after.

It might have taken her longer than was necessary to end up in Logan's bed permanently, but since the moment she said, "I do", she'd thrown caution to the wind. Despite the fact that they didn't have any more rendezvous with another man, the sex was still off the charts explosive as far as she was concerned.

Leaning over, Sam straddled Logan's hips, letting her bare breasts brush against the silky hair on his chest, her nipples puckering from the sensation. Rubbing against him had become one of her favorite pastimes, and quite frankly, she'd begun to wonder if she was a cat in another life.

"Tell me, Logan." Sam encouraged as she scooted further up his body – not down like he would have preferred – until she was straddling his chest and her breasts were inches from his mouth.

Lowering one sensitive tip to his lips, she locked her eyes with his, loving how the hazel depths swirled with uncontrolled hunger. When he latched onto her breast with his mouth, it was her turn to suck in air while her body caught fire.

"Oh God!" It was too good. The feel of his mouth, his tongue swirling around her nipple before sucking harder than she would have thought she liked. "So good."

Sam had learned all of the things her husband liked over the last few months, and she knew how much he enjoyed when she gave him a verbal play by play of how he made her feel.

"Suck harder." She encouraged him, and the flare of pain that flashed from her nipple to her clit proved she had wandered over to the dark side in recent months.

Pulling her breast from his mouth, Sam switched to the other side, watching as his lips slid around her nipple before applying an equal amount of tender loving care to it. She didn't allow him as much time to play because honestly, she wasn't sure she would be able to hold out if he kept it up.

"Sam." His voice was rich and dark with passion, and she knew he was holding on to the very last thread of his control.

"Yes?" She asked again, knowing he was going to get frustrated with her any minute now.

"Honey," he tried for sweet, but failed miserably, "if you don't untie me from this fucking bed, I'm going to break the goddamn headboard."

Grinning, Sam slid down his body once more, making sure he felt exactly how wet he'd made her in the last few minutes. And yes, she wasn't sure how it happened, but somehow she managed to tie him to the bed. It was a wicked fantasy that was proving to be so much hotter than she originally anticipated.

"I'm not finished with you yet." She hadn't been able to convince him to let her tie his legs to the bed, so she was able to use that to her advantage, pushing them wider as she slid off of his body into position between his thighs.

Once again she gripped his erection, ever so slowly sliding her hand over his velvety shaft, enjoying the way he pulsed and throbbed beneath her touch.

"Do you want me to do *this*?" She asked seductively as she tilted her head down and placed a soft kiss on the engorged head.

"Baby." Logan growled. "I'm not playing with you anymore."

"Well, actually I'm the one playing." Sam retorted before slipping her tongue across the slit of his penis, her eyes watching him as he watched her. "Or would you prefer that I do *this*?" She asked before sliding her lips over the smooth head, sucking gently as she pulled him into her mouth.

For the next few minutes, Sam focused on ravishing him with her tongue, using her teeth on occasion to gently scrape the underside which once again had him trying to break free of his bonds.

"Don't you do it." He warned.

Sam chuckled, keeping his cock in her mouth, letting the vibrations wash over him. Oh, she knew she was pushing him too far this time, but if the past was anything to go by, she was going to thoroughly enjoy her punishment.

Logan jerked against the bonds on his wrists, and Sam knew they would give at any moment, so she returned her attention to his cock, using her hand to hold him still while running her tongue down the sensitive underside until she reached his balls.

"Be still. I'm not done." She told him before sucking and licking and torturing him more than she knew he was willing.

"Oh, honey. You're more than done." Logan growled before ripping the scarves that tied his hands and launching himself up from the bed, sending Sam into a fit of giggles before he had her flat on her back.

~*~*~

Logan wasn't quite sure how his wife convinced him to let her tie him down. The gleam in her eye had been so full of promise, and she certainly hadn't disappointed. The problem was he wasn't willing to come until he made her come first. That had become a hard and fast rule that he rarely broke.

When Sam tried to pull away from him, laughing, he gripped her ankle and pulled her closer until he had reversed their roles and he was kneeling between her splayed legs.

"Damn that's pretty." Logan told her as he held her open with both hands, staring down at the soft, pink folds spread before him. "Your pussy's wet, baby."

"Mmmm hmmm" Sam agreed, spreading her legs open wider.

Knowing she liked when he teased slow and easy, Logan decided to give her a taste of her own medicine. He buried his face between her thighs, using his tongue to delve deep inside of her in one quick thrust before emerging and sliding back and forth over her slit, not lingering to torture her clit the way he knew she wanted.

"Logan, please."

The sound of his wife begging was music to his ears. He once again thrust his tongue into her silky hot depths, pushing deep and retreating, over and over as she began to moan and writhe on the bed.

"Logan!"

"Yes baby?" He asked, mimicking the sweet innocence she'd doused him with earlier. "Tell me, Sam. Tell me what you want me to do to you."

"Lick my clit."

She'd gotten confident in the past few months, Sam had. And it turned him on like nothing else. Doing exactly as she instructed, Logan wrapped his tongue around her clit, flicking back and forth over the sensitive bundle of nerves, using his hands to hold her legs apart when she would have tried to trap his head between them.

He might know what she liked, but that didn't mean he was going to give in to the little minx. He had payback on his mind, and at the moment, he wanted nothing more than to bury himself inside her warm, willing body.

"Turn over." He demanded, easily flipping her onto her stomach before she had a chance to argue.

That's another thing he'd learned about his wife in the last two months. She'd gotten bold, thinking she had the upper hand when it came to dominating the bedroom. What she didn't know was Logan would never relinquish full control, and since his brother had ceased to participate in their sexcapades, Logan had been seeking out another man to join them.

Since this was Sam, his wife, and he cherished her more than his own life, he'd been taking his time in determining exactly the right person to join them. What she didn't know... he'd found the man who would soon get the luxury of experiencing heaven as only Logan knew it.

With Sam on her stomach, Logan lifted her hips and aligned himself with her until he was inching his cock into her sweet pussy inch by inch, slow and steady.

"Logan, please!" Sam screamed as she tried to push back against him. "Fuck me, please!" He definitely loved to torture her, but he never could tell the woman no.

Bracing his knees on the mattress and lifting her hips slightly, Logan began to sink inside of her, the velvety soft walls of her pussy clamping down on him, milking him until he was barely a breath away from exploding.

With one hand, he reached around her hip and found her clit. Applying just enough pressure, he pinched between his index finger and thumb as he thrust once... twice... three times before she exploded, his name reverberating through the room.

Logan didn't hold back, ramming into her one last time before his release took him, and the world was suddenly right again.

Chapter Two
~~ ** ~~ ** ~~ ** ~~

Sam walked briskly down the short hallway that led from her office to Logan's. It was past five o'clock, and the second floor was cleared out except for a couple of techs who decided to stay late and look into some of the code they'd had trouble with earlier in the week.

Not wanting to disturb them, Sam kept a steady pace on her path to her husband's office. At work, she tried not to think of him as her husband. She thought of him as the boss, except she didn't work for him directly anymore. Technically.

"Hey." He greeted when she walked through the open door.

"Hey. You needed me?" She asked, recalling the email he had sent a few minutes ago, asking her to meet him.

"I always need you." He smiled that sexy as sin crooked grin that still made her knees weak.

"Cool it, McCoy." She teased as she stepped into his office. "What's up?"

She watched as Logan pulled his keys from his top drawer and then held them out to her. Since they rode together most days, she knew what he was doing, and she wasn't sure how happy she was about it. "When are you coming home?"

Sam knew the routine, knew Logan often needed to stay late for something Xavier wanted, or for a client he needed to meet with. Since it was Friday, she was leery about what type of meeting he might be having, but she wasn't going to ask.

"Give me an hour." He told her.

His gaze was riveted on her, and Sam felt the intense heat snake up her spine the way she always did when he looked at her. For all it mattered, she could have been stark naked standing in his office, rather than wearing her normal Friday casual wear – jeans and a t-shirt.

"An hour?" Logan was always overly optimistic with his timelines and an hour usually meant two, sometimes three. "Well, I think I'm going to stop at Club Destiny for a drink. Ashleigh said she'd meet me there, so why don't I catch up with you at the house in two hours?"

"Perfect." Logan agreed, standing for the first time since she walked in.

The man was utter perfection. Today he was sporting his casual Friday best, which consisted of the expensive slacks he favored and his button down shirt unbuttoned at the throat and the sleeves rolled up. Other than when the man was buck naked, she had never found him sexier than she did at that moment. His dark hair was getting longer than he usually wore it, brushing his collar and the perfect length for Sam to slip her fingers into.

Not that she would be doing that now, no matter how much she wanted to. In the office, she insisted they keep their relationship on the down low. Other than the fact that she was now Samantha McCoy, no longer Kielty, they didn't flaunt that they were married.

Even though her insatiable husband had tried to convince her that christening his office was one of those fantasies he'd always wanted to live out. And each and every time he mentioned it, she graciously refused him.

When he approached, he didn't give her a chance to back away before he pulled her against him and brushed his lips against hers. "I'll see you at home in a little while. I expect you to be naked when I get there."

"Oh, I just bet you do." Sam teased, but there was a glimmer in Logan's eyes that she hadn't seen in quite some time.

"Be careful." He whispered, then kissed her once more, this time more thoroughly than before. "I'll be home in a bit."

With that Sam walked out of his office, keys in hand, and stopped to grab her purse on the way out the door. After calling Ashleigh to confirm their date, Sam was on her way to the car.

Logan watched his wife leave before he picked up the phone and dialed the now familiar number. "Tag. Logan. Hey, man."

"How's it going?" Tag replied, a hint of intrigue belying his cool confidence. "We still meeting?"

"Yes. Only the time and place have changed. Meet me at my office in thirty minutes, if you don't mind."

"I'll be there. I'm actually at the XTX office now. I had to meet with Xavier earlier."

Logan had to remind himself that Tag Murphy had become the man of the hour recently. Since he was a lawyer and now a proclaimed member of Club Destiny, his brother Luke wasn't the only person making use of the man's skills. Xavier had gotten word about Tag and now the man was the newest member of the XTX team. At least as their lead attorney.

"Perfect. I'm in my office. Come this way when you can." Logan clicked the phone off and sat it down on his desk.

This day had been a long time coming. At least since his twin brother Luke had gone off and fallen in love with Sierra and Cole. Since Luke was no longer an option for a third in his and Sam's relationship, and Logan was well aware of his wife's desire to be the focal point of two men since he introduced her to the intimacy of a ménage, Logan had been searching for someone he could trust enough to share his wife with.

Until he met Tag, he'd been worried he wouldn't find anyone. Since he had more background on Tag, thanks to his membership application and Tag's stepbrother Cole's good word, Logan had finally come to the conclusion that he had found the right person to share his wife with.

Logan might be getting ahead of himself because until today, he hadn't yet broached the subject with Tag, which was the reason for their meeting. In the next half hour, Logan hoped he could get a feel for whether the man was open to the possibility or not.

Glancing down at his computer screen, Logan allowed himself to get lost in his emails momentarily as he waited for Tag to show up.

He wasn't nervous, he told himself. What was the worst thing that could happen? Tag could say no? Thinking about all of the ways he wanted to direct his wife's ultimate pleasure, he hoped like hell that wasn't going to happen.

Forty five minutes later Tag was waltzing into Logan's office, a frown on his face. "That boss of yours is a slave driver." Tag joked, shutting Logan's office door behind him before taking a seat.

Logan glanced up at the man and laughed. "That he is."

Xavier didn't have any concept of time, and even though it was Friday night, the man didn't have any qualms about keeping someone in the office if he felt he had business that needed to be taken care of. Logan was living proof – having spent many late nights wanting nothing more than to get home to Sam.

"So what's up?" Tag asked, crossing one ankle over the opposite knee and relaxing into the chair. "No, don't tell me." Smiling, the man continued, "If the grapevine is accurate, I'm guessing this is about your wife."

Grinning, Logan was secretly relieved the hard part was over. "That damn grapevine."

"With a club like your brothers, it's a wonder there aren't some serious rumors flying."

"True." Logan agreed. Knowing Luke worked diligently to ensure the anonymity of his members, the man was the precise reason there weren't more of those rumors running rampant.

"I heard your brother's getting himself hitched, so to speak." Tag offered, allowing Logan the perfect segue into the conversation.

"That's what I hear. Which is the only reason I forgive him for taking his leave from our relationship." Logan halfway joked.

"I've met your wife, Logan. She's a spitfire. Word is she wasn't like that until you cracked her shell when you married her."

If that wasn't the damn truth... Logan remembered the very first day he met Sam. A job interview for the position she currently held with XTX. The woman had stolen his breath from the moment he saw her, and she hadn't let up since.

After a brief time when she felt the need to run from him, Sam finally began to open up to her sexuality and he'd been loving life ever since. Oh, and don't forget she'd said "I do". That was the icing on the cake because with her by his side as well as in his bed, Logan felt as though he could conquer the world.

"I thought *I* was insatiable." Logan admitted. "She makes me look tame by comparison."

"Somehow I doubt that." Tag commented, looking even more relaxed than when he stepped into Logan's office. "Since I'm a member of the club, I think it's safe to say you know more about me than I know about you. And since I know you aren't a man to jump to conclusions about people, tell me what it is you're looking for in a third."

Logan hadn't expected this to be a job interview, but it was what it felt like. "I've got an idea," he offered the man sitting across from him, "Why don't we head out for a beer and I'll clue you in on what I'm looking for."

"You buy, and you've got yourself a deal."

Chapter Three
~~ ** ~~ ** ~~ ** ~~

An hour later, Tag and Logan were sitting at the
bar in a local restaurant, already on their third beer. If they
kept it up, neither of them would be in any shape to drive,
nor would Logan be looking to take Tag back to his wife.
He might revel in the idea of sharing her, but when it came
to her pleasure, large amounts of alcohol didn't factor into
his plans.

Since this wasn't a job interview by any means,
Logan's intent was to get to know Tag a little better, and
vice versa. He didn't plan to talk about their interludes, or
inquire as to the other man's kinks. But he did need to
make sure Tag was compatible with Sam.

In the last hour, Logan had learned more about the
man sitting across from him. A lot more. Like the fact that
Tag Murphy wasn't looking for a relationship, or a
commitment of any kind. That worked out well from
where Logan was sitting. He wasn't looking to bring
another man into his relationship permanently, but he was
looking for someone who could exercise discretion and
one he trusted to see to Sam's best interest.

Before talking to him tonight, Logan knew the basics, including Tag's profession as a corporate attorney. He was thirty four years old, never been married, an only child until his father married Cole's mother, in which he and Cole technically became stepbrothers.

He wasn't from the Dallas area, but nor was he from Oklahoma as Cole was. Being from West Texas, Tag exuded the typical Texas charm, but other than his decipherable drawl, he could have been from anywhere.

"Where's Sam at now?" Tag asked.

Glancing at his watch, Logan had to think about that one. "I assume she's at home or on her way there. She was meeting Ashleigh at Club Destiny for drinks. By her estimate, she'll only be there for an hour, but when she gets together with her friends, I usually stretch that to about two."

"Women." Tag joked.

"Gotta love 'em." Logan stated with a grin.

"Tell me a little more about what you do at XTX." Tag finally spoke a moment later when there was a lull in the conversation.

"I'm the President of Strategic Operations." Logan revealed. "Which means I take a lot of shit from a lot of people."

"I know the feeling. This case your brother's got against Susan Toulmin is wearing me out. Quite frankly, she's one crazy bitch. I mean batshit crazy." Tag offered.

Being that Logan was a silent partner in Club Destiny, and Luke was his brother, he knew all about the case against Susan. The woman had seemingly fallen off her rocker a short while back, filing a lawsuit against Sierra. From the outside looking in, Susan had gotten a little jealous when Sierra landed both Cole and Luke permanently in her bed while Susan had been trying to do the same thing for quite some time.

Neither Luke nor Cole had ever given Susan the impression they were looking for anything more than a romp, but it appeared the woman's greed had gotten the best of her.

"He told me it'll be over soon." Logan added, looking at Tag. "I think we'll all be relieved when that happens. This is hitting way too close to home, and when it comes to Club Destiny's members, they aren't looking to make their membership public, which seems to be Susan's ultimate goal now that she's been outed."

"Well, they don't have anything to worry about. The judge isn't going to ask for the membership list, and I'd fight it tooth and nail if he did."

Logan couldn't say he wasn't happy about that. Being that there were some well-known names on that list, he worried about the fall out. Since Xavier, Logan's boss, wasn't even familiar with that side of Club Destiny, he figured the man might have something to say since Logan, Tag, and Alex were all on that list. Not to mention Xavier's grandson, Dylan, was looking to become a member – though no one knew exactly why at the moment.

A short while later, Tag and Logan decided to call it a night.

"You got any plans tomorrow night?" Logan asked Tag as the two men walked out of the restaurant.

"Not yet, I don't." Tag offered. "Why? What's up?"

Logan knew this was the moment of truth, but if he was going to go through with it, he had to spit it out. "I'm thinking about surprising my wife."

Tag grinned. "I like where you're going with this."

With that, Logan and Tag came to an agreement. Eight o'clock on Saturday night, Tag would show up at his house.

Now Logan just had to come up with a plan. Since he'd had months to think about it, that wasn't going to be all that hard.

~*~*~

The next morning, Sam woke up early, her mind awhirl with things she needed to get done. She was supposed to meet Ashleigh and Sierra for lunch, but before that could happen, she needed to run to the grocery store. For the first time in months, Logan had told her that they didn't have any plans for the night and Sam had decided she wanted to cook for him.

No, she wasn't much of a cook, but she could hold her own. When she put her mind to it, there wasn't much she couldn't at least attempt to figure out.

She ran through the shower and pulled on jeans and a t-shirt before venturing out to the store. Once there, Sam remembered exactly what she hated about the grocery store. Especially on the weekend.

After a miserably long half hour, she managed to make it through the checkout line and back to her car with her goods. By the time she got home, she was starving and ready for her lunch date. A quick glance at the clock confirmed that her stomach was just going to have to rumble for at least another hour.

Thankfully she busied herself by unloading the groceries and planning out her meal. Maybe she should arrange to have dinner on the veranda. They hadn't done that in a while.

Stepping outside, Sam was immediately assaulted by the memories of the times she had spent on the back patio. Specifically the times she had spent with Logan and Luke. Since they were distant memories, Sam wondered how the heat continued to course so brilliantly hot at the reminder.

And to think, those days would never be again. At least not with Luke involved. Not that she wasn't happy for the man, as well as Sierra and Cole. The three of them were truly happy and seeing her brother-in-law absent of those storm clouds in his eyes was definitely a sight to see.

Being that Logan was the easy going one, it was almost strange to see Luke so laid-back these days. Sierra had alluded to some particularly juicy encounters between the three of them, including the use of some of that equipment in Luke's upstairs game room, which explained part of his newfound happiness. Apparently it hadn't belonged to him as everyone originally suspected, but instead he had taken it from one of the abandoned rooms at the club.

From what Sierra said, they were enjoying the use of it from time to time. And if the smile that lit the woman's face was anything to go by, she was much more open to new experiences than Sam was. She could only hope some new opportunities would present themselves soon because despite the fact that her husband could make her all kinds of excited, and fulfill her every need, her experience with ménages had left her with an ache she wanted to satisfy again.

Chapter Four
~~ ** ~~ ** ~~ ** ~~

Logan got home just in time to kiss Sam on her way out the door. She was going to meet Sierra and Ashleigh for lunch, and in turn, Luke was stopping by the house for a little while. Since the two of them hadn't spent much time together, Logan had hoped for just the opportunity.

Tossing some burgers on the grill, Logan took a long pull on his beer as he waited to ensure they wouldn't ignite into a fireball. Once they were cooking, he closed the lid and turned around to see his brother coming out the back door to join him.

"I'm starting to worry about you." Logan told him when he came closer.

"Why's that?" Luke asked, pulling a chair from the table and dropping into it.

"Remember how Grandpa used to say we shouldn't make those faces because we might just get stuck like that?"

Luke turned his head, his forehead creased with confusion, apparently trying to figure out what the hell Logan was talking about. He put him out of his misery. "Well, it looks like you've been smiling too damn much lately and your face got stuck."

"Oh, shut the hell up." Luke laughed, something Logan noticed he was doing much more of recently.

"So, I take it things are still going well?"

"Never better." Luke answered, downing half of his beer. "How could it not?"

True, Logan thought. His twin had finally let down some of those walls he'd erected in order to keep everyone at a distance and after what seemed like a damn long time, he'd finally ended up right where he wanted to be.

"Where's Cole?" Logan asked.

"Alex has him running his ass off. He's at some conference in Austin this weekend."

Logan thought about it for a second and wondered how their relationship worked out. With three people to consider at any given time, he figured there would be some serious jealousy going on when one of them was away. Granted, he never got that impression from any of them, but he still couldn't get his mind around it.

Maybe that was because he was a damn possessive man and when it came to Sam, he wanted to know that she belonged to him and only him. Always. At least as far as her love was concerned.

Sharing her body? Now that was an entirely different story. Only because he wanted to watch the way her eyes smoldered when she was turned on or the way her body ignited when another man touched her. Not that she had been with another man besides Luke since Logan met her, but the memories were enough to make his cock stand tall.

"So how'd it go with Tag?" Luke asked, pulling Logan back to the present.

"Well I think. He's coming over tonight, but Sam doesn't know that yet." Logan watched his brother for any sign of a reaction. When it came to Sam's well-being, Logan wanted to ensure she would never be hurt and if Luke knew something Logan didn't, he hoped his brother would tell him.

"Well, I think Tag's a smart choice." Luke offered, settling some of Logan's nerves.

"Yeah? Why is that?"

"Cole is certainly in his corner, and when he backs you up, you know it's for a good reason. Not to mention, Tag's not looking for anything right now, which makes him a prime candidate."

True. Logan wasn't looking for someone permanent, but he was looking for consistency. He damn sure wasn't interested in sharing his wife with multiple people. Since Tag wasn't in a relationship at the moment, and didn't seem to be engaging in any activities at the club, Logan hoped this could be a repeat adventure for them, but he wasn't going to hold his breath.

"How does Sam feel about this?" Luke asked.

That was a good question, one Logan had given a ton of thought to.

"We haven't out and out talked about it, but I know she's hoping for something to happen. I don't know if she would ever tell me straight out that she wants to bring another man into our relationship, but she hints from time to time."

Especially when they were in bed. Logan had encouraged her to share her fantasies, and it appeared Sam was beginning to think they were his. Sure, he was excited about the pleasure he knew this would bring his wife, but when it came down to it, if she wasn't willing, he wasn't either.

But that was neither here nor there. Tonight they would find out how onboard she was with the idea.

~*~*~

"Well, it's official." Sam stated when Sierra joined her and Ashleigh at the table. "Your glow must be permanent."

That ignited a smile on Sierra's face that warmed Sam's heart. It was good to see her friend so happy.

"I won't disagree with you. I have to admit, I'm having the time of my life." Sierra added as she perused the menu. "I'm starving. Did you order already?"

"No, we've been waiting for you." Ashleigh grinned. "Let me guess, you had to give Cole an appropriate send off?"

Sierra laughed, and Sam watched closely.

"Maybe." She teased then sat up straight when the waitress approached.

The three of them put in their orders and waited
for the waitress to leave the table once again.

"So how are you and Alex?" Sam asked Ashleigh.

"Good. Nothing exciting on that front. At least not
right now."

Sam knew that Ashleigh and Alex were seeing
each other, but for some reason, the two of them weren't
sharing much with anyone else. Not that their relationship
was any of Sam's business, but being that the three of
them were meeting a couple of times a week, Sam was
starting to worry about her friend.

"Where is he?" Sam inquired, glancing over at
Sierra then back at Ashleigh.

"He's at a conference in Austin. Both he and Cole
left this morning. I think my brother's joining them on this
trip as well." Ashleigh offered, but she didn't look happy
about the news.

"How long will they be gone?"

"Until tomorrow." Sierra said. "Alex has been
gone a lot lately, I hear."

Sam knew he had been, she worked for the man.
But she also knew it wasn't always business that was
taking him away, but no one seemed to know what or who
was taking up so much of his time.

"I guess. I'm too busy to notice most of the time." Ashleigh looked as though she wanted to be talking about anything except for Alex, and Sam couldn't fault her for it. If she didn't want to talk about it, obvious from her apparent lie, she didn't want to push.

"So, tell me more about this BDSM equipment that you've got up in your gameroom." Sam asked Sierra, immediately changing the subject for Ashleigh's sake.

Sierra blushed profusely which made Sam smile. "It's interesting, I can tell you that much."

Sierra's lack of detail was a little disappointing, but Sam hadn't made it that far in life by not asking questions. "Have you guys added any more to the collection?"

"Collection?" Sierra's eyes widened. "I wouldn't say that the couple of things we have would constitute a collection, but no, none of us have an interest in that sort of thing."

Sam didn't imagine Sierra needed much outside stimulation when she was currently the filling in one hell of a sex sandwich. She knew from experience exactly what it was like to have two men focused intently on her and even if she only admitted it to herself, she felt a pang of jealousy.

Obviously they were going to dodge topics today because Ashleigh quickly changed the subject, this time talking about her current novel in the works. That was one thing they'd all three gotten used to in the past few weeks. Ashleigh, also known as Ashton Leigh, seemed thrilled with the idea that she now had a couple of people to bounce her ideas off of.

"I need for one of you to explain what it's like to have a threesome." She stunned them both simultaneously.

"Ummm, like in detail?" Sierra asked, glancing to Sam as though she wanted help with getting out of this one.

"Yes."

"Are you telling me that you've never had a threesome?" Sam asked, knowing the answer, but trying to get Ashleigh to talk.

"That's what I'm saying." She confirmed, smiling. "And don't go acting like it's an everyday occurrence. I seriously doubt you had one before you met Logan."

"True." Sam said, but then realized she couldn't very well go into detail because the only person she'd experienced a ménage with was Luke. Since Sierra was at the table, she wasn't comfortable sharing those intimate details. Not that she would anyway.

"Are you considering having a threesome?" Sierra asked, concern written on her face.

"Oh goodness no. Well, not in the near future anyway. I'm in the middle of planning out my next book, and I think my readers would seriously get into the idea of a ménage, but since I don't have a clue what it's like, I can't very well write about it."

"Are you telling me that you have firsthand experience on everything you've written about? Because let me tell you, I've read your books, and some of the things you write about are well past anything I could have ever fantasized about." Sam offered, leaning back when the waitress came with their food.

The three of them had to wait once more while their food was placed in front of them, and their waitress happily checked to see if they needed anything else. As soon as the woman was out of earshot, Sam stared at Ashleigh, waiting for her answer.

"Well, no, that's not what I'm saying. It's just that..."

Sam didn't know how Ashleigh was going to dig herself out of this one, but she was waiting patiently, her grumbling stomach not terribly happy with her at the moment.

"Ok, no. I don't have any experience. I mean none whatsoever." Ashleigh admitted with a sigh.

Was she saying...? Sam's eyes widened as she tried to comprehend what her friend was telling her, but before she could voice what was on her mind, Sierra beat her to it.

"You're a virgin?"

Ashleigh glanced back and forth around their table before grimacing. "Good grief, announce it to the entire restaurant why don't you."

"Oh my goodness." Sierra was apparently out of words.

"Holy crap, Ashleigh. How in the world have you come up with the material you've plied your readers with? I have to admit, I'm addicted to these erotic romance novels you've got going on, but I would have never imagined you could come up with some of that stuff without any experience whatsoever."

"Addicted? Hmmm... I like that." Ashleigh beamed. "It's not that hard really. Just because I've never had an orgasm at the hands of a man, doesn't mean I haven't experienced one for myself." She laughed as she poured ketchup on her plate like they were talking about the weather and not an intensely personal aspect of her life.

"But..." Again Sierra seemed to be overwhelmed to the point she couldn't even finish a sentence.

Ashleigh laughed, but then her smile died a quick and painful death and she looked more than serious, staring back and forth between both women. "Don't you dare tell another living soul. I mean no one. Not Logan," she said, looking at Sam, "and not Cole or Luke," she told Sierra. "Nobody whatsoever."

"Does Alex know?" Sam couldn't imagine what his reaction would have been if Ashleigh told him.

"Good God no! I mean seriously. I'm almost thirty years old. Could you imagine what he'd say if he were to find out?"

No. No, she couldn't.

On top of that, Sam didn't know how the hell Ashleigh Thomas had made it this far without ever giving in to temptation. She did want to be a fly on the wall when Alex found out though. That was going to be comical.

Chapter Five
~~ ** ~~ ** ~~ ** ~~

"How was lunch?" Logan asked Sam when she walked in the door several hours later.

"It was... good."

Logan got the impression Sam was holding something back, but he wasn't about to ask what it could possibly be. She was a woman, and she had just spent several hours with her closest friends. He could only imagine what the conversation entailed, but quite frankly, he didn't want to know the interworking's of the female mind.

He and Luke had talked over their burgers, but they definitely hadn't talked about anything personal the way he figured the girls did when they were together. His conversations with his brother generally consisted of a few sports references, but mostly they talked about the club or XTX.

"So, what's on the agenda for the afternoon?" Sam asked when she tossed her purse onto the table, along with her cell phone. "Is Luke here?"

"No, he left a little while ago. Something about getting home to his woman and taking advantage of having her all to himself."

"Hmmm..." Sam said as she snuggled up against him, allowing him to fold her into his arms. "I like the way his mind works."

"Yeah?" Logan's body went instantly hard at Sam's implication, but he knew that he had to hold her off for a few hours because he wasn't about to interfere with his plans for the evening. "Well, I was thinking we could catch a movie, then come home so you can make me that dinner you promised."

"What'd you have in mind?" She asked as she looked up at him, her arms wrapped around his waist. Logan would never tire of having her touch him, or being able to hold her close. It was the second best feeling in the world, the first of course being when he was sheathed inside of her.

"I'm thinking we should catch up with the rest of the world and check out the Avenger's movie." He told her, placing a kiss on her lips.

"I'm game for spending a couple of hours checking out some hot guys who save the world." Sam's mischievous smile made Logan laugh.

"Is that right?" He asked as he grabbed his keys and wallet from the bar. "Well, I'm willing to let you watch hot guys, as long as tonight, I get to watch you."

Her green eyes darkened with desire and Logan was tempted to turn her toward their bedroom and have his way with her before they went to the movies. When she looked at him like that, he wanted nothing more than to strip her naked and ravish her incredible body. For now he would have to wait.

He only hoped he could withstand the anticipation.

By the time Sam and Logan made it back to the house, he was more than ready for eight o'clock to roll around. So ready, he was tempted to call Tag and tell him to get his ass over to the house.

Sam had tested him for the last two hours, doing wicked, wicked things to him that made him want to strip her naked right there in the movie theater and have his way with her while the whole fucking place watched. The woman was downright evil when she was horny.

What the hell had they talked about at lunch, he wondered to himself.

"Dinner will be ready in thirty minutes." She called out from the kitchen.

At this point, Logan wasn't much in the mood for food, but that was because he was hungry for something else entirely. Figuring he had no choice except to be patient, he ventured outside and turned on the television his wife had convinced him to put out there. He remembered when she had given him a hard time about not having one.

Every now and then, they would sit outside on the patio and watch television, drinking a glass of wine and enjoying the early spring temperature. The best time had been when he'd secretly slipped a porno in when Sam hadn't been looking, trying to surprise her. She'd surprised him right back. Right here on the couch.

Glancing at the pool, he wondered if he should get her in it later. The night was cool, but the water was heated so they could still enjoy it. He'd like it even more if he could convince her to get in naked.

While his eyes stared at the television, he was seeing his wife naked in his mind's eye, only to be interrupted by the sound of his cell phone ringing.

"McCoy." He answered, taking a long pull on his beer.

"We still on for tonight?" Tag's laidback drawl came through the phone.

"We are."

"Perfect. See you at eight." With that, the line went dead, and Logan was once again reassured. Now he just had to figure out how to delay dinner so that they were still in the kitchen when Tag showed up.

~*~*~

Dinner was perfect if she did say so herself. Sure, she might have had to recook the bread, tossing out the original rolls she'd burned and forcing Logan to wait an extra twenty minutes while she put the finishing touches on, but in the end, it worked out perfectly.

They were still sitting at the kitchen table, drinking wine and talking, but something was off about Logan. He seemed distracted, and Sam couldn't figure out why.

"Is something wrong?" She finally asked when he stopped talking altogether.

"Yes."

Her heart thumped hard in her chest and worry filled her mind. She waited patiently for him to continue.

"I think we need to talk about your punishment." He said, sounding entirely too serious.

"For what?" Sam had an idea what he was referring to, and she bit back a grin. Their movie date had been entertaining, to say the least. She'd offered a little payback of her own making while they were seated in the dark theater and she didn't think he'd appreciated it.

"Don't play innocent with me, woman." He scolded her before standing from his chair and taking his wine glass to the counter. When he returned, he took hers from her and deposited it beside his.

Butterflies erupted in her belly making it hard to breath.

"Come here." He ordered, making Sam's heart stutter erratically. She loved this side of Logan – the hardcore, demanding, no holds barred side.

Her feet weren't listening to reason, and apparently neither were her legs because she was unable to push up from her chair. Still sitting at the kitchen table, Sam was rooted in place, watching the sexy way he moved, the glimmer of seductive passion that backlit his beautiful eyes.

"Alright. I can take a hint." He told her as he moved closer, his enormous body looming over her. "If you want to do this at the kitchen table, I'm all for it."

Wait... what? The kitchen table? Surely he wouldn't.

Before she could inhale – or argue – he lifted her easily and deposited her butt on the hard wooden surface. He eased between her legs as he lifted her chin so she had no choice but to look him in the eye. What she saw there lit a flame deep in her core.

"What do you think your punishment should be?"

Sam wasn't sure whether the question was rhetorical or not, but since it was the second time he'd mentioned it, she was thinking maybe not. What should her punishment be? It was a really good question and had her mind whirling with the possibilities.

"I'm beginning to think I should take you over my knee."

Oh God! Surely he wouldn't! The thought of being spanked was humiliating, but just as equally arousing. She had never been spanked before.

"Do you want me to spank you, Sam?" Logan asked, holding her chin firmly in his fingers.

"No." She tried to put some insistence in the single word, which was why she was stunned that it came out sounding more like a question.

"Are you sure about that?"

He was right to question her because she was questioning herself at the moment. Did she want him to spank her? Would he really do it if she told him yes?

"That's it." He said in a tone that heated Sam's skin from the inside out. "Stand up."

Chapter Six
~~ ** ~~ ** ~~ ** ~~

When he took a step back, allowing her room to ease down from the table, Sam did exactly as he said. She couldn't hide the grin, and when she looked up, she saw ecstasy shining in the hazel depths of his eyes while a smile tipped the very edges of his sensual lips.

Logan took a seat in the chair she had vacated earlier and put his hands on her hips, turning her until she was facing him. Sam had to brace herself by placing her hands on his shoulders. His movements were jerky, as though he were excited, which she knew he was.

"Strip."

Logan's terse voice was like a shockwave to her insides, shaking her up and throwing her off balance. Was he really going to go through with this?

"Take your clothes off, Sam." He slowly enunciated each word, as though she hadn't understood him the first time.

Oh, she understood alright. She was just a little on the timid side at the moment.

With her back to the living room, facing Logan, Sam sucked in air and a little bit of courage while she was at it. They played these games frequently, so getting naked in front of her husband wasn't unusual. In the kitchen was a little strange, but not enough to shake her resolve. Apparently she was a little leery of the promise of punishment. Something he'd never done before.

Without further hesitation, Sam slowly disrobed, removing her shoes first, followed by her jeans and t-shirt. Just to push him a little, she left her panties and bra on because she knew he would expect them to come off, as well.

"I said strip. Since when does that mean you can leave anything on?" Logan asked pointedly, his heated gaze caressing every inch of exposed skin.

"Mmmm... Sorry." Sam uttered, trying to appear as though she were. "I forgot what you told me to do."

"Is that so?"

She liked taunting him, liked pushing him because in the end, he would overwhelm her with pleasure. "Yes."

"In that case, I think you've definitely earned your punishment. Come here."

Sam walked to him, taking slow, measured steps, anticipation burning through her.

Logan turned his chair, placing more space between him and the table before taking her hand. When he pulled her close, she instinctively moved to stand in front of him, but he easily adjusted her course until she was standing on his right side.

"Bend over my knee." Logan's voice was deep, laced with promise.

Sam looked down at his knees, then back at him, unable to move from her spot. Ok, so thinking about being spanked and actually giving in to letting it happen were two different things. Maybe she should rethink this entire situation.

Just when she would have taken a step back, Logan gripped her wrist firmly.

"Over my knee, Sam. Now." This time he injected the firm, definitely-not-kidding tone she'd heard before.

Anxiety coursed through her bloodstream, making her feel dizzy but somehow she managed to lean over, her stomach lying across his thighs. It certainly would have been easier if he'd have put her in position himself, but because he expected her total submission, Sam found forcing herself to do as he said to be harder than she could have imagined.

"Damn, baby. You've got the sweetest ass I've ever seen."

She wanted him to get on with it, get it over with because the longer he waited, the more nerve she lost. When his big, calloused hand began brushing her bare butt cheeks, she squirmed. Although she had left her panties on, the thong offered remarkably little cover.

"It's going to look so beautiful after I redden it with my hand." Logan said, his play by play ratcheting up her anxiety. "Is that what you want, Sam? You want me to spank your ass?"

Oh God! When he put it like that, it was a turn on like no other. To think he would actually do it was another thing.

"Tell me." He ordered.

Sam knew Logan liked to be in control, he reveled in her pleasure, which was another turn on, but he would not continue until she gave him the go ahead.

"Yes." She muttered, holding herself up by placing her hands on his calves, her arms beginning to ache from the strain.

"Yes, what?" He asked, still gently gliding his palm over her butt.

"Spank me." The words sounded silly, but the feel of his hand on her thighs, on her butt, kept her from laughing out loud.

Then there was no room for laughter because his hand came down forcefully, causing her to scream from the bolt of pain that ripped through her butt.

He didn't give her time to recover before he repeated the punishment, although his hand landed on her other butt cheek that time. The sting was intense, but the burning sensation was even more so.

"How many do you think you deserve?" Logan asked, patiently caressing her overheated skin.

Did he actually expect her to answer? Sam hoped not because her breath was lodged in her chest and her brain was on overload.

"How many?" His command was urgent, and he punctuated it with another slap to her behind.

"Ten." She threw out the first number that came to mind, shocked at her audacity.

"Ten? Why ten?" He inquired, again stroking her heated flesh with his warm palm.

"I don't know." She admitted. If she'd been smart, she would have said five.

"Count them off." Logan instructed seconds before the next slap landed firmly.

"One." She choked out. That one hurt and that clearly didn't explain the sudden throb between her legs. Was she actually enjoying this?

Another slap, this one in the exact same spot as the last. She screamed and squirmed before blurting out, "Two."

By the time Logan was finished, her counts barely audible, there were tears streaming down her face, and her ass was on fire. Sam was unable to move, hardly able to think for the pain ricocheting through her bottom.

"So pretty."

Sam's back straightened, and she nearly launched up from Logan's lap. Had he not been holding her in place, she probably would have done just that. It wasn't her husband's voice that spoke those words. She tried to turn, but Logan kept her in place, unable to see behind her as a pair of hands brushed over her tender butt cheeks.

Sam couldn't speak, the exquisite feel of the man's hands on her butt, gently soothing the sting. She could feel his body heat on the back of her legs. How had she not heard him come in? Who was it?

She knew instinctively that it wasn't Luke, but who could Logan have gotten and why hadn't he warned her?

~*~*~

"This is what you wanted, isn't it, Sam?" Logan asked, leaning closer to her ear.

Sam was still lying across his lap while Tag had approached her from behind, lowering himself on his haunches as he caressed the reddened skin of Sam's bottom.

Logan's willpower was being tested at the moment, but he wasn't willing to admit it. With Sam sprawled across his thighs, her butt a bright, rosy red from his hand, he was beside himself with need. This was the first and only time he'd ever spanked Sam, but after that little experience, he didn't promise it wouldn't happen again.

"Answer me." He told his wife.

"Yes. It's what I wanted."

That's what he thought. Logan knew those late night talks hadn't been in vain. His wife enjoyed being pleasured by another man, and Logan enjoyed the hell out of watching it. Right now for instance, while Tag was becoming intimately familiar with Sam's backside, Logan was on pins and needles.

"Stand up." Unable to sit still, especially with Sam's upper body pressing against his cock, Logan knew it was time to move to the next phase. Helping his wife to her feet, Logan stood the moment he was free.

"On the table." He ordered, turning her so her ass was on the edge. Lifting, he assisted her in getting where he wanted her to be.

"Now lay back and take off the rest of your clothes." He ordered, taking a step to the side so Tag would have a direct view of her.

Logan watched as Sam's gaze traced over Tag, watching him with excitement in her eyes. He knew she enjoyed this, knew she'd been waiting patiently for months for a repeat performance. And although Luke wasn't the one to join them, Logan felt at ease with Tag. The man seemed to know how this worked, just going with the flow.

When Sam slid her panties over her hips and down her thighs, Tag reached forward and helped to ease them down her legs.

"Your wife is so fucking hot." Tag grumbled, his deep voice resonating through the empty kitchen.

"Now the bra." Logan instructed, his eyes glued to Sam's hands and the stunning body she was uncovering. "She is the most beautiful woman I've ever seen." Logan added.

"Does her pussy taste as sweet as it looks?" Tag asked.

"Ambrosia." Logan said, feeling damn near in awe of his wife. She was absolute perfection, laid out naked on the table like a feast.

When her eyes met his, Logan made sure she could see everything he felt – every ounce of love, respect, and total infatuation.

"Please, Logan." Sam pleaded.

Logan could deny her nothing, and when she looked at him like that, he knew he never would. "Put your feet on the table and spread your legs."

Sam did as instructed, putting her heels on the table and widening her knees so her pussy was open and beckoning. "It's time for Tag to taste you, baby. I want to watch while he eats your pussy."

Logan hadn't been this excited since the very first time he'd shared Sam with Luke. Watching her pleasure was mind blowing; being able to direct it was a gift.

Chapter Seven
~~ ** ~~ ** ~~ ** ~~

Tag didn't appear to require any further direction because he made his way closer to the table, placing his big hands on Sam's small ankles before gliding them up her calves, over her knees and down her thighs. He took his time touching her, likely enjoying the soft, smooth texture of her skin against his.

Logan watched intently, knowing exactly what it felt like to be where Tag was. To inhale the sensual scent of Sam's arousal, the see the dampness lining the soft, pink folds of her pussy, only moments before he was lapping at them.

Moving around to the other side of the table, Logan took each of Sam's hands in one of his and held it above her head, wanting to touch her, but also wanting an unobstructed view of Tag's bald head between Sam's splayed thighs. Her moans were increasing, her body writhing against the hard wooden table, and her eyes were open and locked on the same place Logan's were.

"Does it feel good, Sam?" Logan asked, leaning forward so his mouth was close to Sam's ear, the subtle intoxicating scent of her assaulting his senses and making his cock that much harder.

"Yes. God, it feels so good." Her words of encouragement seemed to inspire Tag because the man used his fingers to spread open her labia, his tongue easing between the folds, tasting every inch, but never delving into her pussy or over her clit, which Logan knew would drive Sam wild.

"Don't make her come." Logan warned Tag. He wanted her wild.

Sam wanted to throttle Logan for that little bit of instruction. What in the world was he thinking? Here she was on full display for both Logan and Tag, her pussy being intently lavished by a highly skilled tongue, and she wasn't supposed to come. In her opinion, that was almost cruel.

Apparently Tag knew the rules because he listened, easily moving his mouth from the place she needed him most to the inside of her thigh. When he began trailing smoking hot kisses over her pelvic bone, then her stomach, Sam had to grit her teeth. She hoped like hell he was going to do something because she was going to burn alive.

When he reached her breast, he plucked her nipple with his finger and thumb, making it pucker and beg for attention. Logan moved to her other side, releasing one of her hands, but she wasn't free for long before Tag twined his fingers with hers, successfully holding her down again.

Sensory overload was a term she had recently gotten all too familiar with, at least since she had met Logan, but right now, with both men latched onto one of her breasts, their hot tongues teasing her, she was at the breaking point. When Tag used his free hand to squeeze her breast before sucking her fully into his mouth, Sam nearly came up off the table. The pain was intoxicating.

She needed to come. Her orgasm was lingering, but not nearly close enough and if one of them didn't do something, she was going to scream.

Logan released her from his wicked mouth, standing to his full height before letting go of her hand. She waited patiently for what he would say next; instead, he said nothing, shooting her a mischievous grin before ripping his shirt up and over his head.

Lord have mercy the man was a sight to behold. All of that tan muscle... those washboard abs and thick, powerful arms made her mouth water.

There were days when Sam wondered how she had managed to land a man as intensely sexy as Logan McCoy. Those thoughts were usually followed by a reminder that she was the luckiest woman on the planet.

Then there were times like now when he wanted to tease her to death, making her delirious with pleasure. In those moments, she just wanted to strangle him. "Logan."

"Yes, baby?" He asked in that innocent tone that drove her mad.

"Make me come!" She screamed, only to have her attention redirected to Tag.

The man was sex appeal at its finest. He'd released her breast and was standing beside the table, staring down at her, making her feel entirely exposed, which made sense because she was laid out on the kitchen table naked.

When he mirrored Logan's actions, pulling his shirt over his head with one hand, Sam looked her fill. Lean and toned, the man was gloriously sexy.

Although he was bald, he had dark hair over the rest of his body. His chest had a light dusting of hair that arrowed down his stomach and disappeared into the waistband of his jeans, and Sam had a sudden longing to see him naked. As far as she was concerned, it was only fair.

"Let's take this outside." Logan said, breaking Sam's attention before he lifted her from the table and carried her through the French doors that led to the back.

The temperature was near perfect, especially considering she was naked. She knew before long it wouldn't matter because her body had overheated twice already, a third time was a given. Glancing up at Logan, she took the opportunity to kiss him, pulling his head down to hers until their mouths met.

Licking his bottom lip, she slid her tongue inside his mouth, exploring, teasing and pleading all at the same time. She needed more, and he knew it. To her surprise, he didn't break the kiss, he laid her on the oversized couch and maneuvered above her, his mouth fused with hers.

Tag was close enough Sam could hear his labored breaths, and feel the warmth of his body heat near her arm. When Logan did break the kiss, he was immediately replaced by Tag and Sam was lost to the new, strange sensation.

His mouth was firm, his lips fuller than Logan's, but there was something much more demanding in him. Yet Sam could feel in the way he thrust his tongue inside of her mouth that he was looking more to give pleasure than to receive it. She wanted to give back.

In a daring move, she sucked his tongue gently; mimicking what she hoped would be the next interlude in this fiercely erotic bout of evening foreplay. When he pulled back, he looked into her eyes, and Sam saw storm clouds brewing in the exotic gray color.

"Your husband's right. You taste like ambrosia."

His dark voice rolled over her, touching every nerve ending and seeping into some she hadn't even known she had.

Sam's eyes met Logan's when Tag stood back up, her body suddenly cold without either of them close. To her delight, Logan had stripped and was standing naked as the day he was born, beautiful and masculine and making Sam's internal temperature raise some more.

"Sit up." He ordered as he came closer, his erection standing tall and stiff from his body, one hand gripping it at the base. "Put your mouth on me."

Sam immediately did as instructed, longing to taste him, to explore him as he watched her. Sam secretly adored giving her husband blow jobs, mainly because he seemed to love getting them. When the head of his cock slipped past her lips, she rolled her tongue around him, teasing the tip before taking him fully into her mouth.

"That's it, baby. Suck me." Logan encouraged her.

Sam could feel Tag's eyes on her, watching her every move as she slowly laved her husband's cock, wanting to bring him the utmost pleasure.

As she tried to remain focused, she couldn't help but watch Tag undress beside her, obviously not one bit worried about the fact that they were outside or that any one of their neighbors could see what they were doing. Granted, the shrubbery was strategically placed to keep prying eyes out, but Sam knew if someone wanted to see bad enough, they'd get a good show. That was part of the intrigue, at least as far as she was concerned.

~*~*~

Logan slipped his hand into Sam's long blond hair, holding her head in place as her mouth bathed him in magnificent, wet heat. He loved having his dick in her mouth, the way she eagerly tried to please him. She was wanton and wicked when she wanted to be, and Logan loved that about her. Hell, he loved everything about her.

When Tag came up beside him, naked finally, Logan moved slightly to the right, allowing him to walk right up in front of Sam.

"Stroke his cock while you suck me." He told her, his body getting harder by the second. He never could hold back when Sam put her mouth on him, and tonight he'd have to break away just to keep from coming.

Gripping her hair more firmly, Logan held her head still as he thrust into her mouth, letting her lips slide up and down his shaft, her teeth scraping him lightly from time to time. When he had met Sam, she'd had remarkably little experience when it came to giving him head, but over the last few months, she'd made it her mission to improve on that talent whenever possible.

He wasn't complaining.

Logan allowed her to take control of the situation for a moment, when she pulled him out of her mouth, her hand circling his shaft, slowly stroking him the same way she was stroking Tag.

"Harder, Sam." Tag said, taking her hand beneath his and squeezing firmly, increasing the pace.

Sam leaned forward placing a light lick to the head of Tag's cock while stroking both of them at the same time. Logan watched when she wrapped her lips around the engorged head and sucked him into the hot recesses of her mouth.

Tag's legs locked, his body going rigid beside Logan and he knew what the man was feeling. Sam's sweet, soft mouth was so generous, so loving, and he momentarily envied the other man.

But tonight Logan wasn't looking for quick and dirty. He wanted Sam to burn bright and hot before the two of them took her at the same time. Oh, yes, Logan longed to be buried in Sam's ass while Tag fucked her wet pussy, but he had a couple of other ideas first.

"Stand up and let Tag lay on the couch." Logan stated firmly. Sam's hands were beginning to work faster, and if he didn't make a change, it'd be too late to worry about anything else because Logan would be coming in her hand.

Chapter Eight
~~ ** ~~ ** ~~ ** ~~

Sam didn't waste any time when Logan told her to get up. When Tag lay down on the couch, Logan helped her straddle his chest, then his head, the man's tongue snaking out to feast on her pussy once again.

"Logan." Sam moaned his name as he came to stand at the end of the couch. From where he stood, he could see the top of Tag's head, but his face was buried between Sam's thighs and she was grinding down on him.

"Tell me, baby. How does it feel?"

"So good." She whispered.

"Is he fucking you with his tongue? Sucking your clit?"

"Yes. God, yes!" Sam screamed.

Logan placed his hands firmly on Sam's breasts, squeezing gently before bending down to pull her nipple between his teeth. He nipped her before sucking harder, pinching the other nipple with his hand.

Making his way back up, he licked her neck before cupping her face in his hands, forcing her to look at him. "It's so hot to watch Tag fuck your pussy with his tongue, baby. I want to watch you ride his cock, take him all the way inside your hot fucking body until you make him come." He told her, watching her eyes light up with excitement.

Logan was going to make her come just from his words alone. The way he held her head in his hands, keeping their eyes locked was thrilling. All the while Tag was sucking her clit, sparks firing through her womb in all directions.

"Then I'm going to bury my cock in your ass." Logan held Sam's head in his hands as she began to grind down on Tag's mouth.

Bright lights began to flash behind her eyelids as her orgasm began to blossom inside of her. Sparks burst forth from her spine, her clit throbbing while Tag skillfully flicked his wicked tongue back and forth, pushing her closer to the edge. She was going to explode at any moment, she could feel the warmth radiating from between her legs, spiraling upward until...

Tag sucked her clit hard, and her body detonated in a rush of light and sound, the tingling sensation ripping through her, straight up her spine until she screamed into the still night air.

"Damn you're beautiful." Logan said, still holding her head in his palms before crushing his mouth down on hers.

"Please fuck me." She whispered into his kiss, her body still throbbing with need, but more so from the desire to be filled completely.

For so long she'd waited for this day, to have her body filled completely while two men fucked her until she was oblivious to anything else. She needed it. The feeling was like a drug, an addiction that she craved.

"Soon. First I'm going to watch you ride Tag's cock."

Those words were music to her ears because although she might not have them both, at least one of them was going to be inside of her.

"Sit on the couch." Logan instructed Tag who was still laying between Sam's legs, lapping at her, bringing her closer and closer to another explosive orgasm. She was too sensitive right now, her body having just ruptured at the seams.

Sam had to move so Tag could get up, and when she did, he easily pulled her back on top of him, his mouth finding hers once more. She wrapped her arms around his neck, holding him close and kissing him back with the fury that was building inside of her. His tongue was hot, and she tasted herself on his lips, smelled the tantalizing scent of sex mingling in the air.

When he gripped her hair, pulling her head back slightly, their mouths separated, and he planted his lips on her neck, licking and nipping as he moved down to her collar bone. She could see Logan in her peripheral vision, standing to the side, watching and giving Tag free reign for a moment.

He took without asking and Sam gave freely, relishing the feel of his mouth on her. He palmed her breasts, squeezing them together as he licked and sucked each puckered tip simultaneously.

"God yes." She moaned as she pressed against his lips, trying to increase the friction, needing that little bite of pain to take her mind off of the need that was building intensely between her thighs.

Sam leaned back, watching what Tag was doing to her as she pulled his head closer, wanting him to consume her completely. The feeling was intense, and as much as she knew she shouldn't want it, shouldn't want this stranger touching her, tasting her, she did. God she did. She wanted him to fuck her into oblivion, sating her body like it had only been sated so long ago.

A few minutes passed as Tag continued to feed on her breasts while two of his fingers had found their way inside of her, spearing her, but not giving her enough to send her into the ether where she longed to be.

"Please fuck me." She begged, not caring which of them heard her or which of them actually did as she asked.

Then Logan was back beside them, tossing a condom down on the couch, which Tag immediately grabbed, unleashing his mouth from her breasts so he could rip open the foil packet.

Sam moved so that he could sheath his cock before she finally, finally was right where she wanted to be.

"Fuck her, Tag. Fuck my wife while I watch. But don't you dare fucking come until I say so." Logan's words were harsh, demanding, and Sam knew he was venturing closer to the edge himself.

Sam leaned over Tag, placing her hands on his shoulders as she slid down the length of his cock, letting her body acclimate to his size. He was huge, longer than Logan, but not quite as thick, but he filled her nonetheless.

Long seconds passed as her body adjusted, allowing him to push further until she was once again sitting on him, the backs of her thighs resting on the tops of his.

"So fucking tight." Tag groaned, and the words sounded as though they were torn from his chest. "So wet. Ride me, baby."

Sam didn't waste another second, lifting and lowering herself on Tag's cock, taking him in deep, then lifting until he was nearly out.

She must not have been doing something right because Tag gripped her hips and began helping her, adjusting his angle until he was thrusting harder, faster than she could go.

"Fuck!" Tag bellowed, his warm breath caressing her face, his deep voice bouncing from the walls. "Baby, I'm going to come if you keep it up."

Sam didn't know what it was she was doing because he seemed to be doing all the work.

"You're so fucking tight. Feels so good."

~*~*~

Logan couldn't wait any longer. He grabbed the tube of lubrication from where he had stashed it earlier, strangling his cock with one hand to keep from coming just from the sight of Sam being fucked.

"Lean into him." Logan told her as he squeezed the cool gel into his hand, coating his cock with it. When Tag moved so that Sam could lean over more, Logan slicked his fingers with the gel and eased them into Sam's ass.

"Yes." She moaned, once again beginning to lift and lower on Tag's cock.

"Slow, Sam." Tag told her, the strain in the man's voice apparent. He was close, and Logan needed to be inside of her when he came.

Logan penetrated her with one finger, slowly fucking her ass as she pressed into him. Sam enjoyed anal sex, so she was used to the little bite of pain now. Not stalling for time, Logan entered two fingers into her ass, before stroking his cock a couple of times and then lining up behind her.

He had to put one foot on the couch in order to better the angle, but once he did, he was able to slide into Sam, feeling the ridge of Tag's cock through the thin barrier inside of his wife. Damn it was tight.

"Lean forward more." He told Sam, pushing down on her back until she was flush against Tag. A little maneuvering put them into a better position, allowing Logan to thrust slow and steady at first, Tag mirroring his movements from beneath Sam.

"Fuck me, Logan. Harder." Sam groaned, trying to rock back into him.

Gripping her hips, Logan did as she requested, he began ramming into her ass while Tag thrust upward, over and over, the two of them alternating until Sam's body tightened painfully around his cock, trying to milk him for all he was worth.

"Fuck. I'm gonna come." Tag groaned, obviously trying to hold out.

"Come for me, Sam." Logan urged, slamming into her once, twice... "Come for me, baby. That's it. Fuck!" Logan roared his release when Tag did the same, both of them lodged to the hilt inside of her as she screamed Logan's name over and over.

Chapter Nine
~~ ** ~~ ** ~~ ** ~~

A solid month had passed since the last time Tag came to the house and Logan could feel Sam getting anxious once again. After Tag had come over for three weekends in a row, Logan figured she needed a break. Apparently not.

For a month, he'd been rocked by Sam's enthusiastic attitude toward sex. Not that she hadn't been a wildcat before Tag came into their lives, but since, the woman was damn near insatiable. Logan was just out of ideas at the moment.

As it would appear after they christened every room in their house, with the exception of the bedroom because Logan refused to allow another man into his bed, they were left with limited options.

But he had an idea, and he only hoped both Tag and Sam were onboard with it. Since Tag was a member of the club, and Sam was since she was married to Logan, he had opted to try that place on for size. What he wasn't sure about was the location – he knew exactly where, but whether Sam would be onboard with it or not was another question entirely.

There was one night a month when the members congregated at the club, generally in the open playroom initially, and by the end of the night, there was an all-out free for all. It was about as risqué as they came and Logan was tempted to show his wife exactly what it felt like to be watched.

He had placed a call into Tag that morning and was on his way to the club for lunch so he could talk to Luke. It wasn't that he needed his brother's permission, but he was curious as to whether his brother was going to attend as well. That might just make Sam's decision for her because he wasn't so sure she'd be interested in watching her best friend have sex. But, she'd surprised the hell out of him on more than one occasion, so he figured he'd better get the details before he went in search of an answer.

Logan walked into the club through the back entrance and found Luke and Cole sitting at one of the tables in the near empty club. The only other people in the room were Kane and Lucie, who appeared to be having a heated discussion behind the bar. He didn't even want to know.

Pulling out a chair, Logan took a seat at the table, not interrupting the conversation going on between the two men. They looked intent, and Logan only hoped nothing was wrong.

"Hey. Glad you got here. We wanted to talk to you about something." Luke stated bluntly.

We?

"What's up?" He asked, glancing back and forth between the two men.

"You know we have the monthly get together, right?" Luke asked.

Great. At least they were already on the topic. "Yeah."

"Well, as you can imagine, Sierra heard about it and now she wants to attend." Cole interjected, sounding as though he were skeptical of the idea. "Luke doesn't see an issue with it."

Shit. Logan didn't see an issue with it either, except for the fact that Sam and Sierra in the same room might not work out the way Logan planned. Women got touchy about stuff like that sometimes.

"She is going to beg until she's blue in the face and you know it. Before it's over, we're going to give in, so I say we just fucking tell her yes now and get it over with." Luke said in typical Luke fashion.

"Well, I can already see that we might have a problem." Logan told his brother. "I was planning to bring Sam."

"Have you talked to her about this?" Cole asked.

Before Logan could answer, Luke offered his insight. "I imagine that if Sierra knows about it, Sam does to. I'm surprised she hasn't brought it up yet, but maybe that means she doesn't want to go."

"That might be true. I don't see that happening, but it might. Let's just say she does want to go. How's that going to work?"

"What do you mean how?" Luke asked sarcastically. "Do you really need a lesson?"

"Oh shut the fuck up. You know what I mean." Logan laughed. "They've become close friends, and you know women. Do you think they'll be onboard if they're both in the room?"

"Shit. He's got a point." Cole said. "Why don't you and Sam wait until next month and Luke can bring Sierra tomorrow."

"I don't think I can hold that woman back for another month. I figure since she and Sierra are at lunch as we speak, I'll likely get an earful about it tonight anyway."

The three men sat at the table for a moment, entirely at odds on how to handle the situation. Logan knew what he wanted, and he didn't know how Sam would react, but if he had any hopes of settling her down even a little, he was going to have to bring her to the club tomorrow night and just let it work itself out.

"What does Tag think about all of this?" Cole asked after a few silent minutes passed.

"I'm waiting for him to call me back. I can't imagine he'll tell me no." Logan told Cole, knowing that his stepbrother was usually game for whatever came up.

"No, I don't see him saying no." Cole agreed.

"What if they want this? What if neither of them cares the other is going to be there?" Luke asked, staring back at Logan this time. "You know as well as I do that there are usually only a handful of couples that show up each time, so it's not like we can keep them from seeing one another, but maybe this is just what they need. Shit, Sierra's insatiable. For a woman who had never been introduced to this lifestyle, she sure seems smitten with all of it."

Cole laughed. "She's eager to try anything and everything. And good grief, I think she's just lucky to have both of us, or she might just never be satisfied. I know I wouldn't be able to keep up with her by myself. Shit, my dick would be broken by now."

That made both Luke and Logan laugh.

"Well, I think we know what the next steps are. I'm going to talk to Tag first, and once he's onboard, I'll talk to Sam. I've got to tell her that Sierra will be there, and I suggest you do the same. I wouldn't want to be left standing there holding my dick when she realizes her best friend is naked and getting fucked just a few feet away from her."

Luke and Cole glanced at one another, smiled. And Logan chose to get up and leave. He had to find Tag or all of this would be moot anyway.

Logan had just pulled out of the parking lot when his cell phone rang. He hit the button to route the call to the Bluetooth speaker. "McCoy."

"Hey, man. It's Tag. Sorry, I've been in meetings this morning. That damn crazy bitch is still trying to force Luke's hand on this." Tag said, making reference to Susan Toulmin.

"No problem. Look, I've got a favor to ask."

~*~*~

"Are you serious?" Sam couldn't believe her ears, and she needed to know more. Why hadn't Logan told her about this? Sierra smiled mischievously back at her as she pushed her plate away.

The two of them had met for lunch because Sierra insisted there was something she wanted to talk about. Since they'd been having lunch several times a week, Sam didn't think anything of it. Their conversations were usually laced with some juicy details of what was going on with their significant others, but today Sierra had thrown Sam a curveball.

"I'm dead serious." Sierra said. "Every month members of the club get together and have an all-out orgy in the playroom. I don't think Luke or Cole wanted me to find out, but once I did, I've been pestering them about it incessantly."

Sam was in shock. An all-out orgy. For everyone to see? She should've been horrified by the idea, not wondering why Logan had never brought this to her attention.

"And they finally gave in?" She asked Sierra, wondering exactly what it would take to convince Logan to take her.

"Yes and no. Luke doesn't seem to be all that bothered with the idea, but I can't say Cole's in agreement. They were going to talk about it today. I don't see them telling me no though."

Sierra's smile was pure sin. The woman had both of those men wrapped tightly around her little finger, and no, Sam couldn't see either of them telling her no either.

"It's tomorrow night?" Sam was going to find a way, come hell or high water, to get Logan and Tag to take her to the damn club.

"Yes." Sierra's sweet smile was suddenly replaced with concern.

"What's wrong?" Sam asked, wondering what could possibly have wiped that grin from her face.

"Do you think it would be weird if we're there at the same time?"

Wow, Sam hadn't actually thought about that. Would it be weird to see her best friend fucking like crazy in the middle of a crowded room? Especially a man that looked exactly like her own husband? Probably not any more awkward than being there in the first place. "I don't know. I don't think it would bother me."

Actually, Sam knew it wouldn't bother her in the least. It was actually kind of a turn on to think of the opportunity to watch Luke and Cole and Sierra. And how fucked up was that?

Obviously Logan had turned her into a nympho.

"You wouldn't find it odd to see me naked?" Sierra asked, not sounding convinced.

"No." That was the truth. From the look on Sierra's face, she didn't feel the same. "It's not like you and I would be together." Sam might be into the whole ménage thing, and she might enjoy the darker, more dominant side of her husband, but she wasn't interested in women.

"True." Sierra agreed, still looking a little shaken up.

"I say we try it. If it isn't what either of us likes, we'll make sure that, in the future, we don't go when the other is there."

"You sound like you're going to make this a routine thing." Sierra laughed. "We haven't even been once."

No, they hadn't. But the voyeuristic side of her was screaming that this was just what she was looking for.

"I think it'll be fun. But Logan hasn't brought it up, so it might take a little sweet talking to get him onboard with the idea." Sam crossed her fingers that Logan was as open with these things as she hoped he was. "I'll call you tonight and let you know what he says."

Chapter Ten
~~ ** ~~ ** ~~ ** ~~

Sam obviously knew her husband. It'd taken some serious, sweet talk, and a little naked time to convince Logan to take her to the club. Now that they were on the way, her nerves were rioting, and her stomach was erupting from the butterflies taking flight. For the last hour she'd been wondering whether or not she could actually go through with it.

"You ok?" Logan asked as he pulled into the underground parking garage of the club.

"Fine." She said, staring out the window.

"You don't sound fine."

No, she didn't. She was a wreck.

Logan parked the car, turned off the engine and then took her hand. Sam turned to look at him and all of the reasons why she was there came flooding back to her. This man made her want things she'd never imagined. He made her body burn hotter than normal and having him by her side made all of the lust seem warranted.

"Let's go up there, check it out and then if you want to go, we'll go. I'll even invite Tag back to the house." Logan offered.

Sam liked the idea of bringing Tag back to the house, but she liked the idea of something different, much more taboo, all the more. Yes, they had some fun when they were at the house, but it was getting a little stale. There were only so many places the three of them could go before they were back in the same place all over again.

"Ok." She found herself agreeing, and then waiting for Logan to open her door. He'd insisted on it so she'd finally given in months before to his need to be a gentleman. It was sweet, and she secretly liked it, but she liked to give him a hard time about it too.

Logan took her hand and led her through the back entrance to the private club. They could've gone through the main doors and then up the staircase to the second floor, but Sam knew Logan didn't want to draw unnecessary attention. She couldn't blame him.

Once they were upstairs, walking down the hallway, Sam's palms began to sweat. Before they reached the end, where the playroom was, Tag came strolling out from the guest room that he rented.

"Hey." He greeted Logan, and a look passed between the two men.

Sam was just about to say hello when Tag backed her into the wall, pressed his impressive body against hers before kissing her senseless. A distraction. A welcome distraction at that. Damn the man was good.

"Hi." Tag's easy drawl drifted over her when he broke the kiss, staring down at her.

"Hi back." Sam smiled.

"Ready?" Logan asked, once again taking her hand in his.

No. No, she wasn't. But this was the moment of truth. All of her pent up fantasies were going to either come true or come crashing down around her in the next few minutes. Either way, she had to get it over with. "Ready."

Tag fell into step beside them as Logan led her the rest of the way down the hall. When they reached the playroom as Logan referred to it, turning the corner, Sam's jaw nearly hit the floor.

The room was filled with people, yet not a single one of them was naked. No, this looked like just a normal get together where people stood talking, eating a variety of appetizers that had been laid out on a table on the far side of the room. For a second, Sam's heartbeat kicked back a notch, returning to normal.

At least it wasn't a sudden, walk right in the room, get naked and get laid kind of get together. That would have likely blown the top of her head from her body. Across the room, Sam saw Sierra talking to Cole and Luke and another couple.

"Hungry?" Logan asked, sounding amused.

"You knew it was like this, didn't you?" Why would he let her think she was walking into a sensual ambush?

"Who me?" The not so innocent smirk on his face answered her question. "Let's go talk to my brother." He said, pulling on her hand.

Sam made her way across the room, following close behind Logan, wondering what she had been so freaked out about. These were just ordinary people, getting together to chat and eat. Nothing kinky going on. At least for the time being.

"I'm so glad you made it. I was worried there for a minute." Sierra greeted but her smile appeared forced. Sam wondered if she was beginning to think twice about this little endeavor.

"Did you think I would chicken out?" Sam asked, trying to sound more confident than she felt. This was definitely strange, even if no one was naked and running around having wild orgies all over the place. The fact that they might made Sam feel a little awkward.

Did she honestly want to see any of these people naked? Granted, watching porn was one thing. Something entirely different than this. These people were... real. Ok, so Sam didn't think the porn people were fake, but she didn't have to worry about running into them downstairs at the club anytime in the near future. And they wouldn't be looking at her naked either.

Tag approached a second later holding a glass and Sam could only hope that it was something strong enough to make her forget what the hell she was doing.

"Vodka and 7." He said as he handed the glass over.

Dear Lord the man was a saint. "Thank you." She would have repeated it over and over if it wouldn't have made her look like an idiot.

"You look a little tense. I figured this might help you relax."

Logan walked up behind Sam and put his arms around her at the same time Luke walked up to Sierra.

Admittedly, both men were a sight to behold. They were by far the tallest men in the room and aside from Cole, probably the biggest. Even with Logan's hair growing just a tad longer than normal, they were still nearly identical, but it was the fact that they were gorgeous beyond measure that made them stand out amongst everyone else.

Sam knew people were watching them, or rather watching Logan and Luke. As far as she knew, neither of them frequented this monthly get together, so the members of the club were likely trying to figure out what was going on. Thanks to Susan Toulmin, the club had been in the news recently, but Luke was jumping tremendous hurdles to ensure the privacy of his members was not disturbed.

"Is it everything you thought it would be?" Luke asked both women, standing behind Sierra while Cole stood close to their side.

Sam grinned. Yes, she had jumped to conclusions and more importantly she'd given herself more credit than she deserved. Wanton and wicked in the bedroom or the privacy of her own home was one thing. Being here, in front of all of these people, was a true test that she was afraid she wouldn't pass.

"Oh, hush. It'll get better. I'm sure of it." Sierra laughed.

Logan brushed up against Sam's back, and she felt the evidence of his reaction to the entire situation. Apparently this was his forte. After all, he did like to watch, so what did it matter if others were watching, as well.

When he leaned down and kissed the sensitive skin of her neck, she forgot for a brief second what she had been worried about.

"Well, I for one can't wait to get you naked." Logan's deep, sensual voice warmed her from the inside out.

"Right here? In front of all these people?" Sam asked, keeping her voice low and controlled. She wanted to make him burn with lust, and if this was what Logan needed, Sam might just rethink the idea.

"See that couch over there?" He asked, turning her in his arms until she was looking at the big, black couch sitting in the corner of the room.

"Yes."

"I can picture you laid out on that couch with Tag between your legs, licking your pussy while you're sucking my cock."

His words sparked a flame in her belly, making her thighs quiver with excitement. She could almost picture it as well.

"I want to feel your mouth on my cock, Sam." He groaned, his hands gripping her waist firmly, his fingers biting into her skin. "Do you really want to do this here?"

Sam heard the unmistakable lust in his tone. He wanted this. He didn't have any qualms about stripping her naked right here in a room full of people.

Glancing around, Sam noticed that she and Logan weren't the only ones getting close at the moment. She wondered if they had sparked the trend or if it had been going on before she got lost in his passionate words.

Venturing a glance at Sierra, Sam noticed she was now crushed between Luke and Cole and the woman didn't appear to have any issues with making out in a room full of people. Cole had his hands around her waist, her shirt bunched up above them, although the only thing showing was her tiny waist.

It was hot as hell to watch.

Then she turned her attention to another couple across the room. These two were much more comfortable with being naked because at the moment, the woman was halfway there. Her shirt was off, and the man was unhooking her bra until her breasts spilled free moments before he was latching onto one puckered nipple with his teeth.

Sam moaned. She couldn't help it. It was like watching porn in 3D, only these people weren't acting, and they weren't worried about what was going on around them.

"Do you, Sam? Do you want to stay here? You have to tell me, baby." Logan stated, kissing her neck and moving to her side so that Tag could press against her other side. They were making sure not to impede her view.

"Damn that's fucking hot." Tag whispered in her ear, tilting her head in another direction where a stunning red head was leaning against a wall, completely nude while a dark haired man was kneeling between her thighs.

It was fucking hot, just like Tag said and Sam pressed against them both, wanting to feel more of them.

"You like watching while she gets her pussy eaten?" Tag asked, gliding his hand down her arm, but still not touching any pertinent parts.

"Yes." She admitted openly.

Logan groaned in her ear. "Tell me, Sam. If you don't, I'm going to carry you out of here and find somewhere private so I can bury my tongue in your pussy."

Oh God! He was going to make her come.

"Then what will you do?" She asked, not wanting to leave just yet, but not committing entirely to getting naked in a room full of strangers.

Logan pressed his mouth to her ear, turning her head back toward Sierra and Luke. Sam gasped. Sierra was on her knees, right there in the middle of the room, and Luke was holding her head as he fucked her mouth.

"Can you handle it, Sam? Can you handle being on display in here? Sucking my cock while others watch?" Logan asked, his labored breathing making her aware of what this was doing to him.

Then he turned her in his arms, fully facing him, palming her head in both hands and staring her right in the eyes. "Tell me."

Sam held her breath, unsure of what she wanted. It was definitely kink in its finest form, hotter than hell, and she didn't want to leave, but her nerves were rioting, and she wondered how she had even gotten to that point.

"If you say yes, I'm going to strip you right now and watch Tag crawl between your thighs and lick your pussy until you scream."

"And if I say no?" She didn't want to say no. She really didn't want to say no.

"Then I'm going to take you to Tag's room, strip you naked and bury my cock in your mouth." Logan whispered. "No one else will touch you. No one except Tag. I promise you that."

Sam hadn't even considered that, but she probably should have. "I want to stay." She finally said, her breathing just as labored as his. "Please, Logan."

Chapter Eleven
~~ ** ~~ ** ~~ ** ~~

Logan knew what she wanted. He knew that Sam wanted to stay, wanted to experience just what it felt like to be watched by all of these people, although he could have told her that they were going to be busy and likely not going to notice much of anything going on around them.

"Turn around." He told her, wanting her to see what was now going on. The smell of sex permeated the air, lust filled moans echoed around the room as couples, or threesomes, or even the five in the far corner, were getting down right dirty.

Logan knew it wouldn't take long, but he had wanted Sam to come in before they let loose. She'd had a moment to acclimate herself and then she had been overwhelmed by the sensuality that penetrated the air like a fog.

Sam turned in his arms, her back against his chest, and Logan put his hand possessively against her stomach, the other over her breasts. He nodded at Tag so he understood they were moving forward. Sam had given her permission, which was crucial up to this point. Logan had warned Tag if, at any time, she decided she wanted to go, they were going to go without question. He had agreed.

Logan nipped Sam's ear. "Look at your friend."

Sierra was completely naked, sitting in Luke's lap in a chair while Cole was kneeling between their legs. Logan had seen it before, but the last time it had been Sam in between the two men.

This time, Sam was a bystander, only able to watch the pleasure that both men were giving Sierra. If the look on Sierra's face was anything to go by, she wasn't concerned about a damn thing other than what those two were doing to her.

Logan moved his hand when Tag reached for the button on Sam's jeans, easily unhooking it before lowering the zipper. Once he began to ease the denim down her legs, Logan took the hem of her sweater and lifted it up and over her head easily. Before her jeans were entirely off, he freed her breasts from the confines of the black lace bra she wore.

He caught the eyes of a few people who were watching them intently and Logan's dick throbbed, all of the blood rushing between his legs, making it hard to keep standing.

"Do you like to watch, Sam?" He asked, nipping her ear lobe. "Do you like to see the pleasure on someone else's face?"

"Yes." She whispered.

Logan turned her head to the side, "See the group over there?"

There was a group of people, five to be exact, who had taken to the couch in the far corner. One woman was on her back on the couch while another was laying over her in the sixty nine position. On each end, there was one man who was encouraging the two women to feast on one another while the man assisted. Each woman was getting licked by two tongues at the same time and the fifth person, another man, was sitting back watching, stroking his cock.

"Oh!" Sam moaned, and Logan noticed her attention was now directed to the man in front of her.

Logan couldn't see Tag, but he knew what he was doing. He was kneeling between her legs, torturing her clit with his tongue. Logan lifted Sam's thigh, opening her further to Tag.

"That's so fucking hot." Logan groaned, holding Sam up as she began to grind down on Tag's mouth. "Watch him. Watch while he sucks your clit, baby."

Sam tilted her head down, and Logan knew she was watching. And so were a couple of others. Sierra and Luke, for one. They seemed to be riveted to what was going on across the room, what Tag was doing to Sam to be exact.

"Tag." Sam groaned his name, trying to push against him.

Logan was standing there, fully dressed, holding his naked wife against him while another man knelt between her legs, using his tongue to get her off. "Come, Sam. Come in his mouth."

Sam didn't need any more encouragement because her body went rigid and she moaned, not quite as loud as normal, but she could be heard by all in the room.

"So sweet. I love when you come for me."

Logan lifted her in his arms and carried her to the far side of the room, away from most of the others, He didn't mind an audience, but he didn't know if he could restrain himself, so the farther away they were the better.

"Undress me." Logan told her as he stood with his back to the room, shielding her somewhat from the wandering eyes of others.

Sam's eyes were wide, but he didn't see fear, he saw ecstasy glowing in the crystalline green. With the hardest part out of the way, Logan didn't know how long they would last if she turned all of that pent up determination on him.

She did exactly as he told her, undressing him with ease before turning to Tag as instructed. Within minutes, she had them both totally naked and she was kneeling between them. Logan hadn't instructed that. As much as he wanted to see it, from here on out, this was her show, even if she didn't know it.

"Suck me, Sam." Tag told her, gripping his cock in one hand and sliding his other hand into her hair. "Fuck yes."

Logan watched, stroking his dick, praying he wouldn't come too soon because this was just too much. Admittedly, he'd never attended one of these, not by himself, and not with anyone else. He'd been intrigued by the idea, but never had he considered it a possibility with Sam. Now he wondered if she even had any limits to her sexual fantasies.

Sam turned her attention on him suddenly, taking the head of his cock in her hot mouth, licking and sucking as she moaned. The vibrations were going to set him off if her talented tongue didn't do it first.

Gripping her head, he held her in place, pushing in and pulling out, letting her tease him with her tongue. And then she turned back to Tag, bathing the man with the same wicked skill and making him groan.

Logan wasn't going to be able to take much more of this. From his peripheral vision, he could see a handful of people, all in various stages of undress, doing erotic things to one another all while his wife was on her knees giving him and Tag the blow job of the century.

Sliding his hand into her hair once again, he eased
her upward, not pulling, but guiding her back to her feet.
When she was standing once again, Logan crushed his
mouth down on hers, stealing a kiss hot enough to melt the
last of his remaining brain cells.

"I need to be inside you." Logan told her none too
discreetly. At this point, he didn't give a shit who heard, or
who watched.

Sam kissed him again, hungrier this time, giving
him her silent approval as she wrapped her arms around
his neck and all but climbed his body.

~*~*~

Sam knew where she was, knew what was going
on around her, but just like every time Logan looked at her
as though she were the only woman in the world, the room
all but disappeared.

With Tag's warm body pressed against her back
and Logan pressed against her front, there was no place
she would rather be than right there in that moment.

Overwhelmed. That was the only word that came to mind as she used her tongue to explore Logan's mouth, her hands to latch onto his hair, and her body to soak up his heat.

"Logan." She needed him more than she'd ever needed him before. Inside of her. Filling her to overflowing until she didn't know where he ended and she began.

She caught Logan's subtle nod toward Tag and a sigh of relief escaped. He wasn't going to torture her any longer. Although Tag had sent an orgasm spiraling through her only minutes before, she was aching to be filled by them. Both of them. At the same time.

Logan took her hand and led her to an empty couch in the corner before pulling her down on top of him.

"Ride me, Sam. Sit on my cock, baby."

His lewd words were the equivalent of the flash point of diesel fuel, igniting every molecule until the fire inside of her burned bright and hot. Not wasting another second, she straddled his hips, sitting up so she could guide him exactly where she needed him.

"Logan." He took her hands in his, holding her up and allowing her to find a rhythm that sent shards of pleasure bolting through her.

Being with him was just as magnificent as always, but being here, in this place, was overloading her circuits. From where she was, Sam could see a handful of people, each of them doing their own thing. The group of five was engaged in an extremely complex situation, something she'd never imagined in her wildest dreams.

Across the room, Luke, Sierra and Cole were doing the same thing Sam hoped to be doing any minute now. With Tag finally joining them on the couch, she was getting closer to where she wanted to be.

"Inside me. Now." She told him when she stopped moving on Logan as he pulled her flush against his chest.

She couldn't speak after that because his mouth found hers in an explosive kiss. The room once again disappeared, and Sam was left with only feeling.

"I've dreamed about fucking your ass, Sam." Tag said as he leaned over her, using his finger to imitate what he would soon be doing with another part of his body.

Sam couldn't help but rock between the invasion in her ass and her husband's cock lodged deep inside of her. It was too much, but not enough.

"Be still, baby." This time Logan caught her attention. "Look at me."

Sam stared down into hazel eyes filled with passion and love, and she knew they were going to have to do something fast. She was losing her nerve the longer they waited, especially when she noticed there were others who were doing nothing more than sitting on the sidelines taking in the whole debacle.

When Tag lined up behind her, his huge cock pushing against her, trying to gain entrance, Sam stilled.

"You love to have your ass and pussy filled at the same time, don't you, baby?" Logan asked, causing her to stare down at him once again. "Move forward."

Sam moved up a little, far enough for Logan to draw one nipple fully into his mouth, and she couldn't stop the scream that broke loose. It was exquisite. He freed one hand so he could pinch her nipple while sucking on the other, and the alternating sensations were intense.

"Tag." This time Sam called out for the man gripping her hips from behind. She wanted him to get closer.

"I'm here, baby." He consoled her as he leaned over.

Pain gripped her momentarily as Tag eased inside of her, Logan remaining motionless beneath her except for his thorough manipulation of her breasts.

Sam glanced around, and noticed the beautiful red head she'd seen earlier, now bent over the edge of a couch, the man behind her ramming hard and fast as he pulled her head back by her hair. She was moaning, and the look of pure satisfaction on her face was enough to send a shockwave through Sam.

When the pain eased, Sam was awash in sensation. Heat bloomed from her core as Logan and Tag began to move in unison, Sam's attention once again focused on her husband. His hand snaked out and wrapped around her head, pulling her down to him. He didn't kiss her though, simply held her face close to his.

"You're the most beautiful woman in the entire fucking room." He told her as he began to thrust eagerly. "Damn your pussy's so tight. Fuck me, Sam. Right here. Right now."

And with that, the rest of the room once again faded into the background, the only thing she could see was Logan. The only thing she could feel was the glorious friction.

"Damn, baby." Tag groaned into her ear. "Your ass is so tight. I can feel Logan's cock inside of you."

Sam could feel it too, both of them, filling her, impaling her over and over until they were moving in unison, one thrusting hard and fast as the other retreated.

Her orgasm rippled, taking hold as a tingling sensation built deep in her womb, her pussy spasming around Logan's cock.

"That's it, Sam. Come for us." Tag urged, holding her hip as he plowed into her over and over.

"Fuck." Logan growled. "I can't hold on."

"Don't." Sam insisted. "Come for me, baby." She urged her husband seconds before her orgasm detonated, taking off like a rocket and barreling through her at the same time she felt both men still inside of her, their groans of release echoing through the room.

Epilogue
~~ ** ~~ ** ~~ ** ~~

[McCoy, Logan – 5:54pm] You almost ready to go?

[McCoy, Samantha – 5:55pm] I need about 30 minutes

[McCoy, Logan – 5:55pm] Ok. Let me know when you're ready.

Logan sat in his office, wondering what in the world Sam was doing on a Friday night. It was the first Friday in quite some time that Xavier hadn't insisted that Logan stay late. That was probably because the man was out of town on business, not expected back until late Wednesday. Logan knew that meant he had the opportunity to get some more pressing things done, but he just wanted to get home and relax for a while.

Sam had come in early that morning because she had an extensive meeting planned, so he figured she'd be just as ready to go home as he was. He couldn't imagine what she was working on. Instead of bothering her, he immersed himself in one of the project updates he needed to modify to present to the board next week.

When seven o'clock rolled around, Logan was just about to walk down to Sam's office when his door opened, and she walked in.

"Hey." He greeted her. "I was just about to come get you."

"Yeah?" She asked as she shut the door behind her. Then a slight click sounded as she locked it.

He could only stare back at her. What was she up to?

"Did you need to talk about something?" Logan asked as she made her way across the room, perching on the edge of his desk in front of him.

"Something." She stated, still sounding very strange.

"Is everything alright?" Logan was beginning to worry because Sam never came to talk to him in his office. She was adamant that they not show any affection to one another during work hours. It wasn't professional, she'd told him.

"It will be." In a surprising move, Sam slipped off her sandal and put her foot on the edge of his chair, pushing him away from his desk.

"What's going on, Sam?" Ok, so he was past the point of being worried.

"Nothing's wrong." She grinned for the first time since walking into his office. "I was just thinking."

"About what?" Logan stared back at her, waiting.

"I was thinking how you work too hard."

"Well, I'm not the only one, baby. It's seven o'clock on a Friday night, and I've been waiting for you, remember?"

"That's not entirely my fault." She told him as she stood in front of him now, between him and his desk.

"No?" Logan saw something in her eyes, something akin to heat, and he wondered exactly what she was thinking.

"No. I've been waiting patiently for the rest of the team to go home."

For what, he wondered.

When Sam went to her knees on the floor in front of him, Logan damn near choked. What the hell was she doing?

"I've been giving some serious thought to that fantasy of yours." She told him as she reached for his belt buckle.

Logan sucked in a breath. He didn't have to think too hard to know exactly which fantasy she was referring to. After all, they were in his office, and his sexy wife had just locked the door behind her.

"Yeah?" He encouraged her to keep talking. He loved when she told him in no uncertain detail exactly what she wanted to do to him.

Once she unhooked his belt, she moved on to the button and zipper of his slacks, expertly easing his now hard cock out of its confinement.

"I've been thinking about how good you taste." Sam said as she leaned forward, placing a kiss to the swollen head, making his dick jump in her hand. When she sucked him into her mouth, he bit back a groan.

Unable to stop himself, Logan gripped her hair, pulling her closer to him as she sweetly loved his cock, licking and sucking like only Sam could do. "What else have you been thinking?"

Sam pulled him out of her mouth, using her lips to plant kisses down the shaft, sliding her tongue against the vein running down the underside, making his balls tighten painfully. If she wasn't careful, he was going to come in her mouth right here.

"I've been thinking how hot it would be for you to fuck me in your office."

Now that was surprising, given all of her reluctance at the office, but Logan was not about to point that out. Not when she was blowing his mind with her tongue. He didn't say more, just held her head in his hand and slid his cock back into her mouth.

"Damn that's good, baby. I love when you suck me." He told her, holding her head still so he could control his movements. "Lick my balls."

Sam did as he told her. She always did as he told her and she made sure he knew how much she enjoyed it. "Oh, damn, baby." Logan groaned as she bathed him in moist heat. "I want you naked. Right fucking now."

Logan's vulgar tone turned her on and made her wet. She'd been battling a severe case of nerves all day as she planned out exactly how this was supposed to go. With Xavier out of town, Sam knew this was her one and only opportunity to give back to Logan for everything he'd given her.

He was the most unselfish man she'd ever met, and after all of the ways he pleasured her, Sam wanted to show him how much she loved him. It had been a huge risk coming into his office, but now that she was here, she wondered how they'd managed to avoid this all along. It was hotter than hell to have him in her mouth while she knelt on the floor behind his desk.

When he pulled away from her, fully expecting her to get naked, Sam did as he said. Within seconds, she had her jeans and t-shirt off and on the floor beside her while he was rapidly doing the same with his own clothes.

"On the desk." He ordered her, and Sam eased up onto the wood, the laminated top cold on her butt.

"Spread your legs, Sam."

Again she did as she was instructed, wondering how in the world the power had changed hands. Sam had fully anticipated coming in here and granting the man this one fantasy, but he'd easily turned the tables.

"Oh!" Sam moaned when Logan buried his tongue between her legs. He was using his thumbs to hold her swollen lips apart, his tongue delving into her. It was erotic, to say the least. She leaned up so she could watch him.

"I'll never look at this desk the same again." He told her as he licked gently back and forth before flicking his tongue against her clit.

"Yes. Right there." Sam told him, wanting him to make her come because if he didn't, she was going to explode anyway, just from watching him.

Logan sucked her clit into his mouth, his tongue tormenting her until she couldn't hold out. Gripping his head in her hands, she held him to her as her clit pulsed and throbbed. And then she exploded, her orgasm a violent pulse inside of her, making her muscles tense as she held his head between her legs.

"Damn that's hot." Logan said as he moved up her body, pulling her bottom to the edge of the desk. Thank goodness he was tall because he easily lined his body up with hers before sliding into her.

And yes, it was hot. Her skin was coated in perspiration, and her breathing was labored. The intensity of her orgasm had damn near drained her, but Logan was working furiously to build the next one that would likely blow her mind.

"Fuck." Logan growled, lifting her legs until they were hanging over his arms. "You're pussy's so wet. So fucking tight."

Logan rammed into her over and over, each thrust harder than the first. The desk was moving beneath her, but the only thing she could focus on was the heat reflected in his eyes.

"Come for me." She told him, trying to take the reins once again. "You're going to make me come, Logan."

Logan leaned over her, pressing her thighs against her body as he fucked her relentlessly. He locked his gaze with hers. "I love you, Samantha."

The words touched her just like they always did. Sam tightened her internal muscles, gripping him as hard as she could. "I love you too, Mr. McCoy."

And with that, they exploded together, Logan's mouth coming down on hers so they could inhale the groans that they wouldn't have been able to stop.

Logan held Sam's hand as they walked to the car. His mind was still racing and he was damn near hard as a rock again, wanting her. She'd blown his mind yet again, but then again, he'd come to expect it from her.

Sam might not realize it, but she had walked into his life and since that day he'd been mesmerized with her. Everything about her. She'd gifted him with her love, and because of that, he knew that he would go to the ends of the earth to make her happy.

"So?" He asked when they reached the car.

"So what?" Sam asked, smiling up at him.

"How in the world do you plan to top that one?"

"Oh, I'm sure we'll think of something." She told him, leaning up to kiss him.

Logan pulled her against him, holding her close and loving every second of having her in his arms. "I'm not sure anything will be as good as that was."

"I'm thinking we should rent a room at the club. That might inspire some ideas." Sam stated when Logan opened the car door for her.

"Baby, I think you're addicted to sex." Logan smiled, then groaned. The woman was going to kill him. And boy what a way to go.

"No, not sex. I'm addicted to *you*." Sam grinned.

Check out more from Nicole Edwards

Club Destiny

Conviction

Temptation

Coming Soon

Seduction

Enjoy an excerpt from TEMPTATION:

Chapter One
~~ ** ~~ ** ~~ ** ~~

"Club Destiny." Luke didn't bother trying to hide the gruff irritation in his voice when he clicked the answer button on his cell phone and all but slammed it against his ear. The damn thing had been ringing nonstop for the last two hours, so he'd stopped bothering to look at the screen before he answered.

"Hey, bro. What's going on?" Logan, Luke's nothing-if-not-persistent twin brother, greeted back, seemingly immune to Luke's umbrage.

Flying under the radar for the last two months had taken some creative manipulation, but Luke had pulled it off, making a full-fledged effort to work on some of his own personal issues. Nonetheless, said personal issues were not resolved, but he found himself right back in the thick of things once again. He shouldn't be surprised that his brother was calling, and he wasn't really, he just wasn't in the mood to talk to him considering the ass chewing he was expecting.

"Not a damn thing. What about you?" He barked back, walking through the main floor of his club on the way to his office.

He'd spent the better part of the morning with Club Destiny's head bar manager, going through their weekly order, and trying his damnedest to get back into the groove. Between that and answering the phone, he hadn't had a minute to himself. Which in his current state was probably not a bad thing.

"Glad you could make it back." Logan said, and Luke heard his brother's sarcasm, as well as his frustration, but at the moment, he didn't give a damn.

"What do you want?" Luke made it to his second floor office and slammed the door behind him.

Thankfully there were only a handful of people at the club that early in the day since they weren't open to the general public yet. Only members were allowed in during the morning hours, and they all knew to give him a wide berth on a good day. Unfortunately for them, today wasn't a good day.

Even with the few familiar faces he'd seen that morning, Luke's only desire was to be left alone. Although he'd managed to abandon his responsibilities, as well as any of his personal relationships for the last eight weeks, Luke still wasn't in the mood to be around anyone, and he wasn't keen on the idea of talking to his brother either.

"What the hell's wrong with you?" His brother never did have a problem calling him to the carpet so to speak, and apparently, Logan wasn't in much of a better mood than he was.

Which was surprising with all that had apparently happened to Logan during the time that Luke had been away. The man was a husband now, for Christ sake. That alone should make his brother much more pleasant than he currently was.

With a silent groan, Luke flopped down into the high back executive chair that he managed to occupy for at least a few hours every day. Glancing around the immaculate office, gleaming with hardwood and soft, iridescent lighting, he tried to remember what made him find comfort in the place.

Oh wait. He didn't.

The oversized mahogany desk, the full size, distressed leather sofa, and the intricate, *way* overpriced designer rug had been someone's idea of soothing. Instead, the result was just fucking ugly. And the confined feeling that overcame him when he walked in didn't help either. Without windows, the not so small space seemed more like a broom closet than an office.

Even after spending thousands of dollars on some highly recommended interior designer, Luke hadn't felt comfortable in the space. Which explained why he spent most of his time down in the club or caught up on the mountains of endless paperwork from home.

Despite his discomfort with enclosed spaces, the club as a whole offered him a sense of peace that was absent from his personal life, thanks to his own demons that managed to haunt him day and night like a bad case of the flu. Rational decisions weren't generally on Luke's short list of things to do, so purchasing the club ranked right up there with one of the best he could come up with in quite some time.

Though he often wondered if the club actually intensified those demons.

Remembering that he still held the phone to his ear, and his brother wasn't going to wait patiently for long, Luke answered. "Just trying to get some shit done around here." *And not succeeding worth a damn.*

Luke almost felt guilty for directing his annoyance at his brother, knowing the other man had spent the last two months trying to juggle his own responsibilities, including a full time job and apparently a new wife, along with covering for Luke's absence at the club. Yes, the wife part had been a surprise because when Luke had left town, Logan and Samantha were only dating. When he came back... *Bam!* – new sister-in-law.

For some unexplained reason, just the thought of Samantha had Luke's body going instantly hard. Most likely that was due to the fact that he'd known Sam intimately, on more than one occasion, thanks to the few times Logan had invited him to be the third. The remembered feel of Sam against him, or her hot, sweet mouth on him, had Luke almost longing for another encounter with her. *Almost* being the key word.

Since his personal demons had begun making a daily visit, Luke had sworn off those little sexcapades.

Granted, Luke liked Sam. And as far as Logan went, she was a perfect match for him.

The fact that they had gotten married shouldn't surprise him as much as it did. Or perhaps the fact that his identical twin brother hadn't bothered to mention that little tidbit of information prior to Luke taking some time off was what kept throwing him off. Either way, he tried not to think about it too much. Especially knowing that what they had shared before could never be again, especially after that last night...

Luke brushed off the thought. He didn't have time to dwell on what couldn't be.

"I'm glad you're back, Luke, but we need to talk." Though Logan's tone was slightly less frustrated than before, Luke easily picked up on the insistence his twin had thrown in for good measure. Luke hated when his brother did that shit. He'd much rather face the anger than to have to face the fact that he had let his brother down.

"Then talk." Luke stated, leaning back in his chair, thinking twice about propping his size 15 boots up on the polished wood top.

He could almost predict what Logan wanted to talk about after all their twin bond was strong, and for most of their lives, they could finish each other's sentences, sometimes even knew what the other was going to say before they said anything at all. And now wasn't much different.

"I'll drop by around lunchtime. Don't disappear on me." Logan stated flatly before the line disconnected.

"Sonuvabitch." Luke mumbled to no one in particular. He might deserve to have Logan show up on his doorstep and read him the riot act, but it didn't mean he was going to be happy about it.

Luke hit the switch to turn on his computer screen so he could scan through his recent emails. While he had been away, he'd managed to stay on top of things as best he could. He couldn't abandon his responsibilities altogether, though he'd been so fucked up in the head that he had wanted to. Even now he had a hard time keeping his focus. So many things had happened in the last couple of months, Luke wasn't sure he knew which way was up anymore.

As much as he wanted to blame everything on what had happened that last night with Logan and Samantha, Luke knew he couldn't do that. Sam might've come into Logan's life, and in turn Luke's, but the woman hadn't done anything specific that would have thrown Luke's life off course the way it had been. No, he only had himself to blame for that, but his own denial wouldn't allow him to admit that either.

"Fuck." Luke ground out as he pushed out of his chair, nearly sending the damn thing over backward. He had too much shit to do to sit around pondering the reasons why he felt so off kilter lately.

He should just leave again, take another extended vacation and get away by himself. Not that it would do him any good. After all, he'd spent the better part of two months doing exactly that and look where it had gotten him.

Not a damn place.

Resigning himself to staying at the club and attempting to take care of business, Luke grabbed an invoice off of his desk and headed back downstairs to talk to Kane Steele, his bar manager. According to their earlier conversation, it appeared that there were some issues with the deliveries while Luke had been away.

Either that or someone was fucking with him and stealing his inventory. Luke didn't even want to contemplate that happening; Heaven help the asshole who would be brave enough to steal from him in the first place.

~ * ~ * ~ * ~

Sierra Sellers wasn't all that enthusiastic with the idea of being set up, regardless of how hot and mysterious – her mother's words, not hers – the man might be. Apparently her mother was under the impression that Sierra needed a date, and rather than asking her if she were capable of finding one on her own, Veronica Sellers had chosen to make her own arrangements. Those arrangements had led to Sierra piling into the backseat of Logan McCoy's supercharged Cadillac CTS while he and his wife talked quietly in the front seats.

After a very brief, very one sided conversation with her mother, Sierra had resigned herself to this outing. Very reluctantly she might add. Veronica's argument consisted of the words "new to Dallas", followed by "essential to network", with the cherry on top of the conversational sundae being "get your business established".

So, no, Sierra hadn't come up with a strong enough excuse not to go along with her mother's logic, though she still didn't understand how a date was going to help her in that regard.

When Veronica had mentioned that XTX – the company her mother worked for – was holding their annual vendors conference in just two days, Sierra hadn't thought anything of it. Why would she? XTX didn't have anything to do with the interior design company that Sierra had yet to even name.

Only when Veronica mentioned that the conference was in Las Vegas had Sierra's ears even perked up. And here she was, on the next leg of this journey that she only hoped would turn out the way her mother intended.

And yes, she was incredibly nervous, despite her reluctance and despite the fact that she felt as though she were being led to an execution. Even armed with a few details about the man she was going to meet, Sierra wasn't feeling all warm and fuzzy about the outcome. The positive side of this endeavor was that she at least knew what the man looked like. Or at least she thought she did.

According to both her mother and Samantha, she was off to meet Logan's identical twin brother. That had immediately piqued her interest because hell, she had to admit, Logan McCoy was smoking hot. Not that she would share that little tidbit of information with anyone, especially the man's wife who she had become close to over the course of the last few weeks.

But realistically, how similar could the two of them actually be? They were grown men for goodness sake, and surely their personalities would set them worlds apart in appearance. So when Sam and Veronica had reiterated the fact that they were identical, Sierra had mentally rolled her eyes and resigned herself to finding out on her own.

Maybe her mother's physical descriptions were accurate. Although Sierra liked Logan enough, she still wasn't all that enthusiastic about the idea of being set up with a man – gorgeous or not. The one positive that she could manage to conjure up from this entire screwed up ordeal was that she and Sam had actually become good friends. Since the woman was the epitome of what Sierra had worked her entire life to become, she knew she would ultimately win in this deal.

At twenty nine years old, Sierra still had some growing to do when it came to establishing herself in business, but after meeting Sam, she knew she'd found a role model who could undoubtedly teach her some things along the way. And when said role model had ganged up on her with the help of Veronica and another woman they worked with at XTX, insisting that Sierra actually meet Luke McCoy, she had found herself outvoted.

Both Veronica and the other woman, Deanna, had spoken very highly of Luke, but something had set her sensors off when Sam had talked about him. If Sierra wasn't mistaken there was something much more intimate about the way Sam spoke of her brother-in-law. Just in case she was imagining things, Sierra hadn't bothered to ask. Not that it was any of her business anyway.

Now, two days later, she was on her way to meet the man, though she got the impression that he had no idea he was being set up.

"You said we were going to a club?" Sierra asked, interrupting the loving couple holding hands in the front seat. "Isn't it a little early in the day?"

"It's a club, but it isn't what you're thinking." Sam offered. "Well, at least not entirely."

Sierra noticed the subtle way Logan squeezed his wife's hand.

What other kind of clubs were there? Besides the ones that offered drinks to people who congregated to laugh, drink and have a good time?

Oh!

Her mind struggled with the possibility before shrugging off the comment. Glancing at her watch, Sierra added, "I didn't realize clubs were open this early."

Eleven thirty on a Tuesday and Sierra was on her way to meet a mystery man who, despite the fact that they didn't know each other at all, would likely accompany her to a four day business conference to be held in Las Vegas.

The Entertainment Capital of the World.

Sin City.

And one of Sierra's favorite vacation destinations.

She could certainly get down with going to Las Vegas, no matter who she was going with. She was quite fond of the city, having gone numerous times for girl's only getaways. Never once had she come back disappointed. Going for business, now that would be a first, but no more so than going with a man. Any man.

What would they do if they didn't get along? How was she supposed to suffer through four long days in the party capital of the world with someone she had nothing in common with?

Granted, she was jumping ahead of herself. She hadn't even met him yet. The one upside to it all, if he looked anything like Logan McCoy, at least she was in for a visual treat.

Logan maneuvered the car into an underground parking garage, and Sierra felt the butterflies take flight in her stomach.

Glancing down, she noticed that she was wringing her hands in her lap, a sheer sign of the tension coursing through her veins. She chalked it up to the fact that she suspected Luke had no idea she was coming or anything else that was in store for him, in the coming days. She'd gathered that from the conversation she'd overhead – ok, more like eavesdropped on – earlier between Logan and Sam. When Logan mentioned that Luke didn't seem to be in the best of moods, she'd momentarily questioned her sanity.

Not that she really cared what kind of mood he was in, as long as he could manage to be polite and courteous for four days, only a few hours at a time while they were in Vegas.

Moments later, Sierra was climbing out of the back seat, coming to join Samantha standing at the side of the car.

"Brace yourself." Sam smiled brightly, looking almost playful.

"Is there something I should know before we go in?" Sierra asked, for the second time questioning what she was walking into.

"Not specifically. Let's just say that Logan's brother is the *darker* twin."

"Darker?" Confusion set in, and Sierra tried to comprehend what Sam was saying.

"You know, mysterious. Ominous." Sam laughed as she took Logan's hand.

Great. Just what Sierra needed. Her mind immediately conjured up a version of Logan McCoy; only this one had a permanent scowl, making him look sinister. She smiled to herself.

With a deep breath, she stood up straighter, adjusted her short skirt, and steeled herself for whatever was to come.

How bad could it be?

21463330R00072

Made in the USA
Lexington, KY
13 March 2013